THE WITCH CHILD

During the reign of Charles I, eight-year-old orphan Jalinda is taken to live with her granny, who is believed by the local villagers to be a witch. When the old lady is drowned on the ducking stool in the village pond, Jalinda is rescued from the same fate by Sir Ralph Frome and his son, Justin. Gradually, over the years, Jalinda and Justin fall in love — but it is a love that cannot be . . .

LYNN GRANVILLE

THE WITCH
CHILD

Complete and Unabridged

LINFORD
(Leicester)

First published in Great Britain

First Linford Edition
published 1998

British Library CIP Data

Granville, Lynn
    The witch child.—Large print ed.—
Linford romance library
1. Love stories
2. Large type books
I. Title
823.9'14 [F]

ISBN 0–7089–5244–5

Published by
F. A. Thorpe (Publishing) Ltd.
Anstey, Leicestershire
Set by Words & Graphics Ltd.
Anstey, Leicestershire
Printed and bound in Great Britain by
T. J. International Ltd., Padstow, Cornwall
This book is printed on acid-free paper

1

I WAS but eleven years old when they first named me for a witch. That terrible day is burned so deeply into my memory that even now there are times when I wake from some nightmarish dream, shaking with fear. Yet it was important, for it brought Justin to me and so sealed my destiny. But perhaps I should start at the beginning . . .

I must have looked a pathetic sight as I stood just inside the door of Granny Fisher's cottage, soaked to the skin by the driving rain which persisted as my companion and I walked the last half mile to the cottage in its lonely isolation at the top of the cliffs. A child of eight, slight and small for my age, my green eyes were stark with misery as I stared at the old woman. Meeting her bleak, unsmiling eyes, I shivered, for her lined face showed no trace of warmth or pity.

My heart sank and I clutched at Mr. Jackson's hand, waiting for her to speak. He glanced down at me with sympathy, then pushed me forward. I was terrified of this silent, old woman and I longed for the comfort of my mother's arms, though I knew I should never feel them about me again. Nor would my father toss me into the air, laughing as I screamed in childish delight. They were both dead and I was alone in the world, except for this woman whom I had never seen before today.

"You say Beth's dead?" she spoke at last. "And her husband, too?"

"Yes, Mrs. Fisher," replied my companion. "Your daughter died of the pox. It was her last wish that I should bring the girl to you."

In the ensuing silence I swallowed nervously, trying to hold back my shameful tears. Granny looked at me suspiciously, her eyes hawklike in the wrinkled face.

"If she died of the pox — why did the child not take it from her?"

Mr. Jackson shrugged his shoulders. "I don't rightly know, ma'am — some say 'tis a miracle." He shuffled his feet awkwardly, then handed her a purse. "This is what was left after the debts were paid. 'Tis not much, there are few folk as will buy goods from a house where the pox has visited."

She took the purse unwillingly. "Is there no one else to care for her? Times are hard and 'tis work enough to keep the flesh on these bones of mine, without a growing child to feed."

He shook his head. "Nay. I'd have took her meself but my wife's dead set against it. I'm damned if I know why. She's a good little thing and she'll be no bother to you."

"Ha! — that's all you know. Children are always a bother whether they mean to be or not. Beth was ever a thoughtless lass. It would not occur to her that I might not want the girl. Not a word from her since she ran off, now she sends me her girl. Well, come here, child, and let me look at you!"

I shook my head, wrapping my arms about Mr. Jackson's knees. He looked down at me with pity and I think he might have taken me back with him had he not feared his wife's temper. Mrs. Jackson was a shrew and she had vowed she would have none of me. He wrestled with his conscience briefly, but he lived in fear of her tongue and he dare not return with me in tow. He untangled my clinging limbs and pushed me firmly into the cottage.

Granny grasped me with her clawlike hands, peering into my face for a long time, a strange expression in her eyes. She sighed. "You're Beth's girl all right. What was that fool name she gave you?"

I took a deep breath. "My name is Jalinda and it is a pretty name. My mother liked it."

"Ha! So you can talk after all. Well, come in, lass. I didn't ask you to

4

come and I dare say as you'd rather be elsewhere — but it seems we've neither of us any choice."

She took my bundle from me and laid it down, then she turned to Mr. Jackson. "Be off with you," she said. "What are you waiting for?"

He was surprised by the suddenness of her attack. He stared at her, then he nodded his head. Abandoning me to my fate, he hurried back down the cliffs the way we had come. I tried not to think harshly of him; it had been a long journey and he had brought me himself. It was more than most would have done.

I stood in the middle of that floor — which was nothing but compounded earth, covered by a layer of filthy rushes — and glanced about me. In one corner was a pile of dried grass which I was later to discover served as Granny Fisher's bed. Apart from a three-legged stool, a coffer, her table and a heavy cooking-pot suspended over the fire I could see only a few bowls and platters.

I recalled the table my father had made, which my mother polished until she could see her face in its gleaming surface. I remembered the stools, the panelled linen-chests, the dresser with its bulbous legs and the special chair which had a high, carved back. It was in this chair that my father sat of an evening, intent on carving the intricate patterns which were his trademark; and taking the same care whether it was something for a valued customer or a little wooden horse for me. The memory of him brought tears to my eyes and they spilled over noisily.

Granny Fisher stared at me, a semblance of pity in her eyes. For a moment I thought she would take me in her arms to comfort me, but she had lost the art of loving. Her life had been too hard and she was too old to begin now.

"Now then, lass, dry your eyes. 'Tis no use in grieving for them as is gone. It won't bring them back and we must think of ourselves. No doubt you're hungry; I never yet knew a child who wasn't."

At this I stopped crying and looked up expectantly. It seemed a long while since I had eaten and my stomach rumbled emptily.

She gave a crow of triumph, her thin lips parting in a toothless grin. "That's it, girl, 'tis time to look to the future. Take off those wet things and come to the fire whilst I make you something to eat. We'll manage, you'll see. It will be hard at first but you'll learn. Oh, yes, you'll learn all right!"

★ ★ ★

And learn I did!

I learned what it was to be cold and hungry in the long winter which followed. I learned to go searching for driftwood on the beach when it was freezing cold and a biting wind blew in from the sea; to come home to the cottage soaked to the skin and to a stewpot containing only a few vegetables — unless we were lucky enough to catch a rabbit. That was seldom enough, for Granny rarely caught anything in her snares — it had been a hard winter for the rabbits, too.

I do not know how I survived that first year. I had been gently reared, and according to the laws of nature I should have sickened and died. Instead, I thrived. I grew thin but it was a tough, wiry leanness.

It was a hard life, so different from the one I had known. Often I would take out the little wooden horse, stroking its smooth surface lovingly. Then I would ache for the sound of my father's voice, or the touch of my mother's hands as she tucked me up in my cot at night. If only someone had shown me a little love, but there was no one but Granny, and she had forgotten how.

Sometimes we huddled together in front of the fire, listening to the howling wind. It tore at the cottage walls with a vindictive fury, and the wares lashed at the foot of the cliffs, sending spray high into the air. On certain nights, when the power of the storm was at its height, I sometimes thought I could hear the souls of drowning men, screaming in the darkness.

"The sea be terrible cruel," Granny said once. "I lost a man and two sons out there on just such a night as this. Aye, she be a wicked mistress, the sea . . . "

Looking at her then I began to understand what had made her the way she was. Loneliness and suffering will make granite of the softest heart in time, and I guessed that her life had been lonely. I drew closer to her, realising that she hated the howling wind as much as I. Somehow that knowledge robbed the storm of some of its power to frighten me and I no longer felt quite so alone.

★ ★ ★

I had been at the cottage for six months when I first saw the house, or, rather, I saw the gates leading to the estate. Huge iron spikes, flanked by stone pillars topped with a pair of eagles. They perched with beaks menacingly open, their wings unfurled as though ready to attack the unwary intruder. So real were they that I almost believed them the guardians they appeared to be.

"Where does that lead?" I asked Granny, pointing to the path which wound into the trees.

"'Tis Sir Ralph Frome's land. He lives in the house beyond the wood."

"Have you ever been there?" I asked, made curious by the tone of her voice.

"Aye, once."

I waited in vain for more. "What is it like?" I persisted.

Her face was troubled as she looked at me. For some reason she was reluctant to satisfy my curiosity. "'Tis big," she said, "grey stone like these pillars and there be strange carvings above the arches in the walls. 'Tis an accursed place and you'd do well to keep away from it . . . "

Her voice had risen shrilly and she seemed angry. I asked her why she was so upset and why she had been to the house if she believed it an evil place, but her face took on a closed, secretive expression and she shook her head at me.

"Never you mind, girl. Just remember my words, no good can come to you from that place . . . " She broke off, her eyes dilating with fear. Suddenly she gripped my shoulders, her fingers biting into my flesh. She seemed to look through me at something only she could see, studying my face as though trying to discover the answer to some mystery. Then she shook her head again.

"I can't see . . . 'Tis not clear . . . "

"What is it, Granny, are you ill?"

My question appeared to break the spell. She started, a dazed look coming into her eyes. "What? Ill, you say? No,

I'm not ill. 'Tis nothing, nothing at all . . . " She frowned, glancing up at the dark clouds gathering overhead. "'Tis time we were going home — we've picked herbs enough for today."

She hurried me past the forbidding gates with their fierce guardians. I went reluctantly. My curiosity had been aroused and I longed to squeeze through the thick hedge which bounded the estate. Granny had warned me against the house but she was always warning me about something, the list was endless. Usually I obeyed her without question but this time I could not help thinking that there would be no harm in just looking at the house — from a safe distance, of course. However, I was careful not to let Granny guess that I intended to return one day — alone.

She was in a hurry to get home before the storm broke and she forgot the incident almost at once. There was work to be done, she said. I knew that meant she would be up half the night, boiling the herbs and berries we had collected in the big black pot over the fire.

Granny understood the wild plants and berries. She made a potion which was supposed to cure anything. It smelt vile and tasted worse, but she swore it was the secret of her long life and she drank some every day. She made me drink it too, but whenever I could I poured it away.

Sometimes she took a pitcher of it to a house in the village, just as dusk was falling, and knocked at the back door. When the door opened a man would glance anxiously down the street to ensure that no one was watching, before snatching the pitcher from her and thrusting some coins into her hand.

Once I asked her who he was but she told me to mind my tongue. It was not until long afterwards that I discovered he was the apothecary. He sold Granny's mixtures to the villagers, pretending that he had made them himself. But when I asked her why she didn't sell her cures to the villagers herself Granny got very cross and said that it was better the way it was.

★ ★ ★

I grew taller and brown like a gipsy as spring turned into summer and summer into autumn.

Sometimes, with a kind of envy, I watched the children from the village laughing and playing together. They would run on the beach and climb the cliffs, but they never came near the cottage. One day, driven by the desire for friendship, I called out to some of them. But as I approached they screamed and ran away.

"Don't be frightened," I cried. "I only want to talk to you."

A dark-haired boy, older than the others, took a step towards me, a friendly grin on his face. But his friends pulled at his sleeve.

"Come away, Tom!" one of them said. "Her granny's a witch. She'll turn you into a toad if you play with her."

"Please don't go, it's not true," I said, but I could see he half believed them.

His face paled and he hesitated momentarily, then he turned and ran away down the hill. I stared after him, brushing a tear from my cheek. I wasn't going to cry. Who wanted to play their stupid games anyway? Holding my head high I walked away, their cruel taunts ringing in my ears. I had something more important to do than wasting my time playing children's games. It was at that moment that I decided I would find a way through the hedge which divided Sir Ralph's estate from the common land.

The thought of that house tantalised me. Granny had forgotten it; she had warned me against going there and believed the matter ended.

Perhaps it would have been if the children had allowed me to join in their play, but they had turned away from me.

★ ★ ★

I visited the gates several times before I managed to get inside the grounds. The hedge was thick with sharp thorns which scratched my flesh, making it impossible for me to squeeze through. I searched hard for a gap but the hedge was kept in good repair and it seemed impenetrable. Then I found the way in by accident.

I was lying in the long grass, enjoying the warmth of the sun on my face, having given up my search for the day. Perhaps because the air was so very still, without the slightest breeze, the fox did not catch my scent. He passed me so closely that I could see his glittering eyes and long, pointed muzzle. His ears were erect, his head tilted to one side as though listening for something. I must have moved, for he became aware of danger and took fright. He made straight for the hedge and vanished.

I stared at the spot where he had disappeared, thinking that he was skulking in the long grass. But though I watched for some time, he did not reappear. At last I decided to investigate and walked towards the place where he had vanished so abruptly. I gazed at the thick wall of hedging, feeling puzzled. Then I saw the flattened grass and a tingle of excitement ran up my spine as I realised that this was the answer to my problem. I could not get through the hedge, but I could crawl underneath it!

I fell to my knees and pulled frantically at the grass and debris concealing the tunnel. It was definitely there, obviously used regularly by foxes and other animals. I searched for a sharp stick to help me clear away some loose earth, digging furiously until I had enlarged the hole sufficiently for me to crawl through. Then I lay flat and slowly wriggled my way beneath the hedge. It was surprisingly easy, but then, I was small and thin — and very determined!

Reaching the other end I stood up, looking about me excitedly. I was in a wood but the trees were thin and there was a track leading through the undergrowth. Leading to what? That was why I had come, I wanted to see the house beyond the trees; the house Granny had described as evil.

I found a large stone, placing it near the burrow so that I would find it easily; then I set off through the trees, noticing the deep pink flowers of the willow herb and the pale yellow spikes of agrimony. I thought of picking some for Granny but changed my mind: she would be sure to ask me where I had found them and I did not want to lie to her.

It was pleasantly cool in the wood. I lingered, laughing as a red squirrel bounded up the trunk of a tree and a woodpecker peered at me from its home in a hollow oak. So entranced was I that I suddenly came upon my objective without realising it. The trees had thinned out and before me was a meadow and a small stream. I looked beyond to the rise where the house stood out magnificently against the sky. The last rays of the evening sun had turned its walls to a rosy pink, and the light was reflected in the tiny windows a hundred times. It sprawled over a vast area of land, dominating the landscape with a kind of gloomy grandeur which enthralled me. In my innocence I thought it the most beautiful house in the world and I longed — oh, how I longed to live there! It was so big, the walls so stout that I thought I should be safe there from the howling wind which shook the cottage: safe, loved and warm.

A rumble of thunder made me look up at the sky; dark clouds had appeared from nowhere and a storm was brewing. The light was fading rapidly and I realised that I had been staring at the house for ages, lost in my dreams. Granny would be worrying about me, I was never away from her for this long. I began to run back the way I had come as it started to rain.

It was dark when I reached the cottage, soaked to the skin. Granny was watching for me anxiously from the doorway and she pulled me inside.

"Where have you been, you wicked girl?"

"I was playing and I forgot the time. Please don't be angry, Granny, I didn't mean to worry you."

"I asked you where you had been. Look at you — look at your dress!"

It was caked with mud from wriggling back through the burrow. I met her eyes defiantly, knowing that there was no point in lying. There was never any point in lying to Granny.

"I went to look at the house."

She did not need to ask which house. Her face tightened with anger and her lips drew into a thin line. "I warned you," she said, "and you disobeyed me. You are like your mother, wild and foolish. But I won't have you bring shame on me — I'll teach you to mind me, my girl!"

She fetched a thin birch-twig from the corner. I whimpered, backing away as I saw her hard face. "No, Granny — please . . . " But she meant to punish me for my wickedness; seizing my hair so I could not escape, she began to lay about me with the switch. Feeling the first stinging blow I screamed, twisting and wriggling in an effort to escape her. Her chest heaved and her eyes glittered as she brought the stick down again and again, thrashing me without mercy until she was exhausted. I collapsed in a heap on the floor, my face stained with tears and hurting all over.

Then I felt her touch my shoulder and I shrank away, expecting more blows, but her voice was surprisingly gentle as she said: "There, child, I shan't beat you any more. Let me smooth some ointment on your back to ease the pain."

A flash of spirit made me angry. "I don't want your help. You are cruel and I hate you. I hate you!"

"Better you should hate me," she said, her eyes sad, "than tread the path of evil."

"You are a silly old woman!" I cried. "You called it an accursed place but you lied. It's beautiful."

She looked at me. "'Tis you I'm thinking of, child. 'Twas to save you pain . . ."

I turned my head aside. What did she mean? She had just beaten me and now she wanted to save me pain. She was cruel and hateful and I wished I was dead.

★ ★ ★

The months passed. I did not die; I went on growing, fast. My clothes began to split at the seams and reveal too much of my long legs.

"You grow so quickly, Jalinda," grumbled Granny, "and where's the money coming from to buy new clothes, tell me that?"

"Perhaps you could sell some more of your cures?"

She sighed, shaking her head at me. But soon afterwards she went out gathering herbs and that night she made up potions and creams which I had never seen before. The next morning she packed them into a basket and we carried it down to the village.

It was market day and the village was crowded with folk buying and selling their waves. Granny selected a quiet position in a corner of the square, but she did not call out as the other women did. She merely set out her pots and waited.

Soon a man came sidling up to her, his eyes swivelling furtively as if he was afraid that someone was watching him. He whispered to her and she pointed to a jar. He picked it up, thrust some coins at her and scurried away. She smiled coldly and beckoned to me. Pressing three pennies into my hand, she pushed me in the direction of the stalls.

"There you are, child, take it and spend it."

I stared at her, unable to believe my own ears. She couldn't mean I was to spend it as I liked — could she? Astonished, I saw that she did.

She laughed. She actually laughed! The first time I had ever known her to show real pleasure in anything. "It is for you, to do with as you will," she said.

I wasted no more time, speeding into the thick of the crowd, my fortune clasped in my hand, half afraid that she would call me back. I doubt I would have heard her if she had, I was too busy planning how to spend my amazing wealth.

The sun was warm and I soon lost track of time as I wandered about, weaving my way through the crowd. We seldom came to the village and I was fascinated by the sights. I saw a man bartering a horse for a cow and calf, another having his tooth drawn. I pressed my hands to my ears to shut out the sound of his screams. Then I saw the man selling strange figures carved of wood. I examined them curiously, wondering what the creatures with long claws and ugly faces were supposed to be.

The man grinned at me, guessing my thoughts. "They be dragons, missie," he said. "Fire-breathing dragons like I seen in foreign lands."

I stroked one, thinking of my three pennies. "How much is this?" I asked.

"How much have you got?" he asked, his wide grin revealing the blackened stumps of rotting teeth.

"Three whole pennies," I replied, full of my own importance.

"Threepence, eh?" He laughed. "Give me a kiss to go with it and it's yours."

Momentarily I was tempted, perhaps because the carvings reminded me of my father; but I disliked the look of him and the foul smell of his breath.

I shook my head, darting away as he laughed mockingly.

I was hungry now and I had seen a woman selling hot meat-pies. Finding her stall, I pointed to the smaller ones. "How much are they, please?" I asked, my mouth watering in anticipation.

"Well, mistress," she said, smiling, "these big ones be sixpence and these be only threepence."

"I'll have a small one, please."

Talking my money, she handed me the pie. I thanked her and went to find Granny. I broke the pie in half, biting in to it as I ran. It burnt my tongue but it tasted delicious and I did not feel the pain.

Granny was waiting for me. She looked tired and drawn. I smiled at her shyly, offering her the other half of the pie. "I saved it for you," I said.

"For me? No, child, it's yours. 'Tis seldom enough you get a treat."

"It is for you," I insisted. "We share everything."

She looked surprised but pleased too.

Then she took the pie, eating it without another word. When she had finished she smiled, saying: "I did well today, child, now we are going to buy you a new dress." I stared at her, open-mouthed. "Don't stare so, why do you think I made all those cures?"

"To buy me a new gown?"

She nodded. "It was the only way, and 'tis not before time. What you have on is hardly decent." She frowned, muttering: "God save it brings no harm — but I had to do it. I had to!"

"Harm, Granny. What harm?"

Her face closed up. "Nothing for you to worry about, child. As for me, well, my time's coming soon enough . . . "

I did not understand. She often spoke strangely and I soon forgot her words in the excitement of buying my new dress. It was not exactly new. Granny bought it from a woman who sold second-hand clothes. It was too big, but I could pull in the waist with the girdle. I did not mind, at least I should not split the seams for a while.

Besides, it was a pretty shade of blue and I liked it.

The business of the dress finished, we bought some fish and a side of bacon. I looked at Granny thoughtfully. If she could earn so much from her cures — why didn't she come to the village more often? But I did not ask her. I knew she must have a good reason; she always had a good reason for what she did. Besides, I was tired and happy and I was only a child. I could not know that she had broken a lifetime's rule to buy me my dress — nor could I have guessed what terrible results it would have!

* * *

It was obvious immediately that our visit to the market-place had somehow changed things. People started to call at the cottage, coming at night and speaking of their business in whispers. At first Granny sent them away but they came back again. In the end she agreed to make the cures for which they asked. She seemed ill at ease, for ever grumbling to herself as she worked. And she would not let me watch her; it was if she wanted to keep her secrets from me. I might never have learnt the truth, had it not been for her accident.

It happened as we were scouring the fields for herbs. She slipped on a piece of rotten wood, hidden in the grass, wrenching her ankle and crying out in pain. I ran to help her and she managed to hobble back to the cottage. Fortunately, her ankle was not broken, but it was very painful and by morning it had swollen to twice its normal size. Poor Granny could not even hobble about the cottage. She sat on her stool, muttering to herself angrily.

"'Tis no use!" she declared at last, "the child will have to do it."

"I'll help you, Granny. I can see to the fire, cook . . . "

"Listen, girl, and stop chattering.

You will have to make something. I shall tell you what to do and you must follow my instructions exactly."

"Yes, of course I will. What are we going to make?"

"Mind your own business, there is no need for you to know. Just do as you are told!"

I looked at her resentfully. I only wanted to know what I was making — why did she always have to be so cross? I am sure that she would never have revealed to me what it was I made that day. However, as the hours passed, her ankle began to throb and she drank some of one of her mixtures and lay down to sleep. So it was I who answered the door to the pretty, young woman who came just as the light was fading.

"Where is Granny Fisher?" she asked, alarmed.

"Granny is sleeping."

"What about my potion — I can still have it can't I?"

My curiosity had reached bursting

point. I just had to know what she wanted so badly. "Yes, of course. Now, let me see — which one was yours?"

"The love potion!" she cried impatiently. "That scheming Jenny thinks to steal my Jed, but I'll show her! With Granny Fisher's spell he will not be able to resist me — but it must be tonight!"

I stared in astonishment. So that was Granny's secret: she was a witch and those children had been right! I hurried to fetch the mixture, taking her money in a daze. My head was whirling madly. If Granny was truly a witch, how many more secrets must be locked inside her brain?

A witch. What power, what thrilling visions the very name held for me! I wondered why she was so reluctant to use her powers, and I thought of all I would do if I had her knowledge. Perhaps it was now that I began to sow the seeds of the misery I was to reap in the future.

It did not begin yet. For several months I continued to live with Granny, but her fall had taken its toll and she was never to be the same. Increasingly, she came to rely on me, and it was thus I learned the secrets she had guarded so long.

Sitting in her corner by the fire she watched me with troubled eyes. At last she broke her silence and told me all I wished to know, confessing that she was a white witch and had learned the art from her grandmother many years ago.

"'Tis not every generation has the power. Some have it, others do not. My daughter did not possess it, nor my mother. But you have it, Jalinda. I guessed it from the beginning — and I feared it."

"Feared it?" I repeated, surprised. "Surely it is good that is exciting to be able to do so much . . ."

"No!" she screamed at me. "You

must never think of it like that. It is a curse on us — a cross that we must bear. It sets us apart from other folk, and sometimes we suffer for it . . . "

I did not notice the flash of fear in her eyes, for I was filled with a strange rapture. "We are different, yes, but that is because we have power . . . "

She gasped, horrified. "Never seek to use your skill for the sake of power. 'Tis only for helping others and must be used wisely — else you will bring evil on yourself."

I solemnly promised to obey her, but inside I was tingling with excitement. I looked at Granny with pity. She was old and her life had been too hard; mine had just begun and I knew it would be different. I was going to make my power work for me. I did not intend to spend all my days in this hovel — I wanted to live in a house with stout walls that turned to rose pink in the sunset.

I think Granny regretted then that she had taught me any of her spells.

But it was too late; I already knew so much. Besides, she needed me.

Soon after our talk I began to notice a change in the folk who came to our cottage. Once they had been ready to stop and chat, now they were anxious to leave quickly. I thought they sometimes seemed frightened. Granny did not notice anything, but then, she was changing too. Her movements were slower, her speech often slurred. She would sit staring into the fire for hours. I had to push her food into her hands, else she would leave it untouched. Once she had cared for me, now I was the cook, the gatherer of herbs; and it was I who brought the trouble on us.

The night I found a stranger at our door I could not have known what was to happen. He looked a poor creature, ill at ease and nervous. He asked for Granny but I told him she was asleep and inquired the nature of his business. He eyed me strangely.

"Well?" I asked, disliking him. "I have not all night to waste!"

He sneered at me. "No, 'tis full moon tonight — the time when witches are busy."

No one had called us witches before, except the children. I wondered what he meant. I had no need of a full moon for what I had to do, but I nodded my head as if agreeing.

"If you want something, sir, say so and let me be about my work!"

His cold eyes made me shiver. "'Tis like this," he said, "I've a wife already, but I like another lass better. What must I do?"

I could not think what he meant. "The only way you could take a new wife . . . " My voice trailed away in horror as I realised that he was asking for the spell of death. "You can't mean it! We do not kill folk: we help them!"

He glared at me, hatred burning in his eyes. "But you could — if you wanted to?" he persisted.

I hesitated, remembering Granny's warning; but my foolish pride let me astray. "I can do anything I want," I boasted, "but I don't like you. Go away, you horrid man!"

He smiled queerly, triumph in his eyes. "I suppose you could make old Simeon's pond dry up and his cows die . . . ?"

I thought he was mocking me and I lost my temper. "I could even turn you into a toad," I cried childishly. "Go away, you nasty man, or I will!" I giggled and waved my hands at him. He turned pale, backing away, terror in his eyes. Then he began to run back down the hill, towards the village. I was triumphant at my victory. What a strange, foolish man he was. As if I could turn him into a toad! I shut the door and went back to the fire.

Granny looked up. "What was all that about?"

I shrugged. "Oh, some horrid man who wanted a potion to kill his wife."

Her face turned grey. "God have mercy!" she cried. "You did not agree to make it, girl?"

"Of course not. I told him we do not make such things."

"'Tis what I have always feared. But it may be safe if you sent him away — you did send him away, Jalinda?"

"I told you so. I don't understand — what is wrong?"

She began to rock back and forth, clutching her arms about her thin body and moaning. "Terrible things can happen to such as we . . . I'd hoped to die in my bed, but I'm old . . . 'tis the child." The rocking motion became more and more frenzied as she repeated the words over and over again. "The child . . . I must protect the child . . . "

She went on and on until I thought I should scream. I asked her what troubled her, but she seemed not to hear me. Suddenly she got up and went over to the coffer, delving inside it to bring out the small purse containing the coins we had earned with our cures. She pressed it into my hands and sat down again.

"Tomorrow, you must go," she said.

"Go where? Why must I go? Please tell me what is the matter?"

She stared at me, her eyes wild. "How do I know where you must go? I've done all I can for you. It isn't safe for you here. You will have to leave in the morning."

"But you can't manage alone!"

"It matters not, Jalinda. I shall die soon enough — one way or another."

She shivered. Her face was grey with fear and I began to feel frightened too. I had boasted so foolishly to that man, and somehow I knew it would mean trouble for us. But I could not leave Granny to face it alone, whatever it was. I did not know why she was afraid, for she would not tell me; but I knew as surely as she that 'it' was coming and that 'it' would be something bad!

They came for us the next morning, a dozen or more of the folk I had thought our friends. In the past they had thanked me often enough, but today their faces were hard and cruel.

I trembled as the sound of angry voices drew nearer, bringing Granny to the door. I could see she was fully aware of the danger.

"Go quickly!" she warned, pushing me out of the cottage.

"No — what about you?"

"I know you don't want to go, child, but you must. I want you to go — now!"

Suddenly I was seized with panic and I started to run away from that angry mob. Then I heard a terrible scream and I looked back. They had caught Granny by her long hair and they were dragging her along the ground. I ran towards them, shouting: "Leave her alone. Oh, please, leave her alone!"

A man was bending over her limp body, but at the sound of my voice he looked up; his eyes burning with hatred. It was the stranger who had called at the cottage last night.

"There is the witch's spawn," he cried. "Take her too — we'll be rid of them both!"

Too late I realised my mistake. I should have kept on running as fast as I could, for what could one small girl hope to do against that blood-hungry mob?

I darted away down the cliff but I tripped in my haste and he caught up with me. He twisted his fingers in my tangled hair, bringing tears to my eyes. I bit him and kicked out wildly. He hit me violently, knocking the breath out of me so that I ceased to struggle. I looked at Granny. Her eyes were closed, her face deadly white. She did not move, even when they bound her wrists and ankles.

They took us to the village. Then a silence descended as they all looked to their leader, waiting for him to tell them what to do next. As he stared at me, his face excited and cruel, I felt my skin prickle with fear, but I was determined not to show him how frightened I was. I lifted my head proudly and faced him. For a second I thought I saw a flicker of fear in his eyes, then he turned away. He pointed to Granny.

"That one first — then the young one."

"Don't hurt her any more," I cried. "She's old and she never did any of you any harm."

I looked at them appealingly but they ignored me — he had them in thrall. They hung on his words, eager for the excitement he had promised. He ran his tongue over his cracked lips, enjoying his moment of power.

"Stick the witch," he said, his eyes glittering, "see if she bleeds. Then you'll know that I speak the truth, my friends. They are evil creatures — they must be torn out of our midst before 'tis too late!"

There were cries of approval then another voice said: "Duck her, that's a fairer test."

At this there was a general murmur of agreement. I gasped, horrified as I realised what they intended. Their faces were masks of cruelty, their voices the grunting of animals.

What happened next is imprinted so deeply in my memory that I shall never forget it — even if I live to be a hundred! They dragged Granny over the rough ground, not caring that blood was oozing from a gash on her forehead. Then two of them sat her in a strange object beside the pond — it was like a stool on the end of a long pole — and they bound her to it so that she could not escape. I saw her head slump forward and a trickle of saliva ran down her chin, but she made no sound. She seemed unaware of what was happening to her, half dead already. I wanted to close my eyes but they were glued to her face. I watched as some of the men went to the other end of the pole, putting their combined weight on it. I screamed as the stool rose high into the air, then plunged down into the icy water.

Their leader grinned at me. "Don't worry, witch — your turn is coming."

I was silent then, biting back my

screams as they continued their cruel work. Again and again they plunged her down into the water; sometimes leaving her beneath the surface for minutes on end. I cursed them bitterly. If I was a witch, then every one of them should die — but nothing happened and they went on with their foul task. At last it was over. They untied her limp body and dragged it across the grass, leaving it sprawled in an obscene heap.

"Now for the other one," my enemy cried.

I waited silently as they came for me. I was numbed, blinded by unshed tears. I did not struggle as they laid hands on me, merely looking at them with contempt. I saw fear and shame in several faces and some of them fell back, suddenly silent. I believe their blood-lust was sated — but my enemy was determined that I should die. He thrust aside those who hesitated and picked me up. I was easy for him to carry, for I was still slight and small.

He sat me in the stool, tying the rope around my waist, gloating as he saw me flinch. Yet still I remained silent, and it angered him. He spat in my face, willing me to show some emotion other than contempt. But I refused to let him see that inside I was desperately afraid. So he turned away, going to the end of the pole and putting his full weight upon it.

I was swung high into the air, then slowly out over the pond. I closed my eyes, terror forcing the scream up through my chest and out of my mouth. I heard his laugh before I was plunged down into the filthy water. I struggled wildly, tugging at the ropes which bound me, feeling the air draining from my lungs. I knew that I was dying.

Suddenly I was back in the sweet sunlight. I gulped the fresh air frantically, coughing and spluttering before I descended into the pond again. But to my surprise, I found that the ropes were being untied and I was lifted gently in someone's arms. I opened my eyes, gazing up into the face of the youth who was holding me. I blinked, thinking he was an angel with his soft, fair hair and his blue, blue eyes. I had never seen anyone so beautiful and I believed that I was in heaven.

"Am I dead?"

He laughed, revealing his white teeth. "No — though it's no thanks to these devils!" He glared angrily at the silent crowd. "You should all be ashamed! She is only a child."

They huddled together, shamed and guilty. It was as if they had only now realised what they had done. Then their leader stepped forward.

"You don't know her, sir," he said, his voice humble. "You live safe in the big house — you haven't seen the evils she and her granny wrought. They are both witches and you'd best let us finish the work."

"Superstitious nonsense!"

I turned to look at the man who had spoken. He sat astride a huge black horse, surveying the scene with disgust. His face was stern just now, anger making him appear proud and cold, but I could see he was my saviour's father. Their eyes were the same blue and they both had a kind, sensitive look. The man smiled at me, waving his hand expressively.

"Wrap your cloak around her, Justin," he said, seeing that I was shaking with cold. "We shall take her with us — there is no telling what they'll do if we leave her."

"Yes, Father." Justin smiled, throwing his cloak about my shoulders.

I returned his smile. Then my eyes travelled to where Granny lay sprawled on the ground, just as they had left her.

"Granny . . . ?" I whispered.

His eyes clouded. "We were too late to help her. I am sorry . . . "

His kindness was my undoing. The tears I had held back flowed down my cheeks. Then a woman came forward. I recognised her: she had been to us for a cure for her sick child.

"I knew Granny Fisher — she lived up there on the cliffs. I know her granddaughter, too, sir. If they be witches — then they're good ones." She looked at me with pity. "Don't worry, child. I'll see as your granny's buried proper."

"Did you say her name was Fisher?" asked the horseman.

"Yes, Sir Ralph." She curtsied to him respectfully.

He looked at me, a glimmer of new interest in his eyes. "You will attend to the burial and look to me for the cost," he told her.

"Yes, sir."

He nodded, his eyes flickering over the silent villagers. "As for the rest of you — you may think yourselves lucky to escape a flogging. If this happens again I shall have the guilty ones whipped and put in the stocks — do you understand me?"

They stared at him, some sullen, others ashamed, but none dared to answer him back.

"Come, Justin. Let us go home before she dies of cold."

The crowd moved back as he turned his horse. Justin swept me up on the saddle, folding his arms about me as we followed. It was then that my enemy cried out:

"You will rue this day, Sir Ralph Frome! She will bring bad luck to your house, mark my words. She is the devil's spawn — a witch child!"

Sir Ralph did not bother to turn his head — but I did. I stared at my granny's murderer and all my hatred was in my eyes. I cursed him then. With all my heart I wished that he would die. He looked into my eyes and the colour drained from his face. His hand went to his throat, as if it was slowly closing and his eyes rolled in terror. I knew he believed himself doomed. I smiled in triumph. Then I turned away, leaning against the warm body of the youth who held me in his arms.

"We will soon have you home," he said, holding me closer. "Tell me — what is your name?"

"Jalinda."

"What a pretty name," he said.

It was then that I began to love him.

2

SO I came to Hallows; the ancient home of the Fromes. Once it had been a monastery and it still showed signs of its origins, though successive Fromes had rebuilt parts of it. But the chapel remained much as the monks had known it, preserved throughout the generations. For when King Henry VIII dissolved the monasteries he gave it to one of his courtiers, little dreaming that the man was a secret Roman Catholic.

The generations had come and gone. The religion of England changed from Catholic to Protestant, returning briefly to the old ways in Queen Mary's time. But from the reign of Good Queen Bess it had remained Protestant until the present day. Now, however, there was a French Catholic queen at her husband's side on the throne of

England, and a king who was tolerant of her beliefs. But now, too, there was a new religion being slowly brought to life; a sterner, stricter code, a breed of men who would tolerate nothing but their own high standards, and already there was unease in the land.

But I knew nothing of these things as I saw that grey stone sprawling house which had filled my thoughts so often. Never in my wildest dreams had I really believed I would ever live within its walls. As we drew nearer I could see the mellowed beauty of the stonework and the strange carvings Granny had mentioned. I thought it wonderful, magnificent in its imposing grandeur. Later I came to think of it as a dark, lonely place, vast and full of secret corners where memories could lie in waiting to twist and stab my heart. But that was years afterwards, when I was no longer a child.

That first day, however, I had no doubts at all. I had been saved from a cruel death and I was going to the home of my fair-faced angel. For me it was enough to be near this young man who had already aroused deep feelings in my breast. I suppose at that time it was gratitude; I was but eleven and I had not yet come to know what I was capable of as a woman. How soon it turned into a blind obsession that I mistook for love I do not know. But even then I adored him.

It was Sir Ralph who took charge on our arrival, while Justin merely set me down and smiled at me. It was his father who sent servants scurrying to dry me, feed me and put me to bed. To me the smile was all, Sir Ralph's concern for a common village girl, nothing. And I recoiled in horror as I heard him tell a stern-faced woman to bath me and scrub me well. I knew not what he meant, but I felt instinctively that I should not like it.

Nor did the preparations for my ordeal change my mind. I watched suspiciously as a big, wooden tub was dragged before the kitchen fire and filled with hot water. I had been ducked once today and in my opinion that was more than enough. I backed away, screaming.

The woman — who I came to know as Mrs. Beeson, Sir Ralph's housekeeper — clicked her tongue, frowning at me. "What the master means by bringing home the likes of you, I'll never know," she declared. "But he has and he wants you clean, so it's in that tub with you — or no dinner!"

I stopped screaming, looking at her. Did she mean it or was it an idle threat? I decided that she was not a woman who spoke lightly and I reluctantly let her remove my gown. She led me towards the tub and suddenly my hunger disappeared: dinner or not, nothing was going to get me in that water!

I screamed as loudly as I could, and I had a healthy pair of lungs. The noise I made could be heard all over the house; sufficient to say that it brought both Sir Ralph and Justin running to investigate.

Sir Ralph frowned at me as Mrs. Beeson explained why I was screaming, but Justin laughed and before anyone could guess what he intended, he swept my thin, gawky body up in his arms and dumped me unceremoniously in the tub. I stopped screaming, sheer surprise holding me silent. How was my idol fallen! That he should do something so outrageous had not occurred to me.

He was amused by my indignant face, but he hid his smile and apologised. "I am sorry, Mistress Jalinda," he said. "But if you want to live with us, you must be clean. I am afraid you smell — it must be the pond water."

Justin was ever the courtier.

At once I was all smiles, my outrage forgotten. If Justin wanted me to be clean, then how ever great the ordeal I would bear it. I submitted to Mrs. Beeson's ministrations without more ado. Justin watched for a while, a smile of approval on his face, and I thought that I would do anything to please him.

When I reflect on our relationship, I can see that it was at that moment I mistook the nature of my hero. His behaviour that day was unlike him, and I have since come to believe that he acted on impulse in a boyish, funning way. But to me he became a bold, courageous being, tantamount to a god. I did not discover my mistake until it was too late.

But now I was resigned to my fate, and Justin and his father went away, leaving me to Mrs. Beeson's none too gentle care. She had been told to scrub me and scrub me she did! I came out of that tub with my skin pink and glowing — a far different colour to when I went in. Once the scrubbing was over, she treated me kindly enough, wrapping me in a blanket and bringing me a plate of mutton-pie. It was a long time since I had tasted anything as good and I ate hungrily.

She shook her head at me, scolding

me for bolting my food, but I was sure I detected a hint of pity in her eyes. When I had finished eating, she led me up some stairs, ushering me into a small but comfortable room. She told me to get into bed and as I slipped between the sweet-smelling sheets I began to think that I was truly in heaven. I had never before slept in a real bed and when Mrs. Beeson drew the heavy curtains which hung from the carved tester I felt so strange that I almost cried out. For a while I lay tense and trembling as the terrible events of the morning crowded in on me, making my mouth go dry with fear and hot tears scold my cheeks. I felt lonely, miserable, and I longed to be back in the cottage with Granny; but I was exhausted, the bed was soft and soon I fell into a deep sleep.

When I awoke it was morning again. Drawing back the curtains I jumped out of bed refreshed and, with the resilience of youth, ready to face whatever awaited me. I thought that even if I was not dead, I was indeed in paradise; for there, waiting for me to put them on, were a body and kirtle of some rich material that was smooth and warm to the touch. Beside the gown, which was a deep red colour, lay a girdle of woven gold threads and a pair of leather slippers.

I touched them reverently, hardly daring to believe that they could really be for me; but as I hesitated Mrs. Beeson came in bearing a smock-petticoat and a falling band of cutwork lace. She motioned to me to put them on and I hastened to obey. I had no need of persuasion this time.

I was not sure how the garments should be worn, for I had never possessed more than a simple gown. However, Mrs. Beeson helped me, fastening the girdle round my waist and arranging the falling band across my shoulders so that the strings tied neatly at my throat. She stood back to observe the effect with a strange look that was somewhere between suspicion and satisfaction.

"H'm — that explains it," she said at last.

"Explains what, Mrs. Beeson?" I asked, puzzled.

"Never you mind, miss. You are to come and eat your breakfast and then the master wants to see you."

After I had eaten, Mrs. Beeson led me to a part of the house I had not seen before. Today I was rested and my natural curiosity reasserted itself. I looked about me, thinking how grand it all was. The furniture was solid with rather ponderous carving and the chairs had thickly padded seats. The walls were of panelled oak, sometimes covered with rich tapestries; and above the great fireplace in the hall hung swords and shields of a bygone age. But I was not allowed to stop and stare; the housekeeper hurried me to a room at the end of the hall and knocked at the door.

A voice invited us to enter. She

pushed me inside, dropping a curtsy as Sir Ralph turned to look at us. I returned his gaze, really seeing him for the first time. He was a fine, big man. His hair was light brown, a single lovelock falling delicately on the exquisite lace ruff around his throat. He had a thin, pale face and a little, pointed beard which he stroked as he regarded me thoughtfully. I felt shy and awkward in my new clothes until he smiled, then I saw his eyes were kind.

"You have done well, Mrs. Beeson," he said. "You may go now."

"Yes, sir," she said, curtsying again and looking inquiringly at me as if asking whether she should take me with her.

He shook his head. "You may leave Mistress Jalinda with me."

He smiled at me again and I smiled back. I was fast losing my fear of him and, growing bold, I made him a curtsy as I had seen Mrs. Beeson do. It was a little shaky and not very elegant but it made him laugh and I knew he was pleased with me.

"Good, Mistress Jalinda," he said. "You are willing to learn and that is excellent for you have much to learn. Come — I shall take you to meet Thérèse and Selina; they are to be your companions now."

I curtsied again, making a slightly better performance this time. His mouth twitched as if he wanted to laugh, but he merely held out his hand and I took it shyly. He asked if I was rested and hoped that I had taken no harm from my soaking the previous day. I replied that I was well and he was silent for a moment. His next words surprised me.

"And your mother, Mistress Jalinda? Is your mother dead?"

I wondered why he should ask me such a question. He seemed sad, remote, as if his thoughts were far away, distanced by time and place.

"Yes, sir. My mother and father both died of the pox when I was eight years old. 'Twas then I came to live with Granny." My eyes clouded with tears as I spoke of the woman who had loved me in her way, though she had never shown it in a conventional manner. I had loved her too, but I had not known it until yesterday.

He saw the look in my eyes and his fingers closed over mine. Clinging to his hand, I felt comforted and safe, almost as though I had known him all my life. He was kind and reminded me of my father, but only because of the way his eyes seemed to smile. They could have nothing in common: Sir Ralph was a gentleman, my father was only a poor carpenter.

Sir Ralph led me up some steep stairs and along a narrow passage. This was part of the old buildings and the walls were rough hewn and damp to the touch; but, after we had walked the length of what seemed to me endless corridors, he stopped and opened a door, standing back to let me enter. The room was large with great arched ceilings and mullioned windows. A huge oak bench stretched the length of one wall, and a log-fire was burning in an open grate, occasionally sending little spirals of smoke into the room. But what drew my attention were the people seated around the fireplace; they had been talking, but as we entered they became silent, turning to look at me.

The man was in his middle years, pale, with sad, gentle eyes. He did not interest me much and my gaze rested curiously on the two girls. One was of about my age and she had soft, fair hair like Justin's. The other girl was darkhaired and a little older, her face quiet and serene. She came to meet us with a smile of welcome in her brown eyes.

"You have brought us Mistress Jalinda," she said in a low, sweet voice. "I bid you welcome, mistress."

I curtsied to her and she clapped her hands in delight.

"This is Mistress Selina," said Sir

Ralph, frowning at the other girl. "Thérèse — come and meet Mistress Jalinda." It was a command not an invitation.

She came but I could see she was reluctant, and her eyes held a look of cold disdain. She curtsied to me; a deep, elegant, graceful movement which made a mockery of my efforts.

"You are welcome, Mistress Jalinda," she said; but her tone belied the words. "I am Thérèse Frome and Mistress Selina Howard is my dearest friend and companion."

Her words were gracious but I felt they held a message for me alone. She was saying that she was forced to accept me because it was her father's wish, but I would never be her friend as Selina was.

"Come — sit with us," she invited. "Mr. Renard is instructing us in Latin."

I stared at her open-mouthed. I had no idea what she meant, but the mere fact that I was to be permitted to stay with them and not banished to the kitchen satisfied me.

"No, no," said Sir Ralph, laughing. "Not today, Thérèse. Jalinda is not yet ready to begin the Latin. She has to learn how to write her name. I shall keep her with me this morning, and Selina may teach her some letters later — if you will, my dear?" He looked at Selina inquiringly.

"Of course, Sir Ralph. I shall be happy to do so," she replied.

I thanked her and she smiled, saying she hoped I would be happy at Hallows. I replied that I was sure I should; then Sir Ralph took my hand once more and we left them to their studies.

I stayed with him for most of the morning and he took me on a tour of the house, showing me the various rooms and explaining the uses of the strange and wonderful things which aroused my curiosity. I had never before seen a looking-glass, nor a virginal or a spit-jack for roasting whole oxen over the fire. I asked questions and he answered them all with a tireless patience. I admired the fine tapestries and pictures, confiding shyly that I had seen nothing like them in all my life.

"Do you like the pictures, Jalinda?"

"Yes, they are lovely."

"Tell me — which one do you like best?"

He watched me walk slowly along the row of pictures, studying them carefully. I halted in front of one that appealed to me. It was a country scene with horses, dogs and a lady talking to a gentleman. "This one — I like this one best," I said.

He nodded, looking pleased. "You have good taste," he said, "that was painted by a fine Dutch artist."

"Dutch artist?" I echoed. "What is that?"

"Who is that?" he corrected. "He is a man by the name of Van Dyck."

"He is very clever," I said, my young face serious.

He laughed at my innocence. "Yes,

as you say, he is very clever. You seem interested, my dear — would you like to know more about these . . . ?" He indicated the other pictures with a wave of his hand.

"Yes, please," I agreed eagerly. I could think of nothing better than to spend my time with him in such wonderful surroundings.

His eyes were warm as they rested on my face. He placed his hand almost lovingly on my head. "Then you shall, child. I will teach you. Now we must return to Mistress Selina; it is time you began your lessons. Promise me you will be good and obey her. We want none of yesterday's behaviour — do you understand me?"

I saw that his face was stern. I knew then that if I wanted to keep his favour I must be obedient and try to learn everything he wished me to know. It would be difficult sometimes, but in future I would hide my true feelings behind a meek face, because I wanted to stay here in this house where there were fine clothes for me to wear and plenty of good food to eat. And Justin — especially Justin!

We returned to the room we had visited earlier. The sad-faced man had gone and the two girls were seated on a bench by the window, sewing with brightly coloured threads on canvas. I was fascinated by Selina's work; it was delicate and pretty.

"You are clever, Mistress Selina — like Van Dyck," I said.

She looked inquiringly at Sir Ralph. He stroked his beard, smiling. "Jalinda learns quickly — you will have no trouble teaching her her letters."

I looked at the pretty threads. "May I learn how to sew like that?" I asked.

Selina laughed at my eagerness. "Certainly you may learn to embroider, Jalinda — if Sir Ralph does not object?"

He inclined his head eloquently. "I would not impose on your free time too heavily, Mistress Selina, but I wish you will do all you can for Jalinda."

"Of course, sir, it is no trouble to me," she replied, giving him a confiding look which showed she knew he meant I had more to learn than reading and sewing.

* * *

And so from that day on Selina took me in her care, teaching me not only my letters, but also how to behave in a gentleman's house. To her I owe my pleasant way of speaking and my elegant bearing. I learned to read and to write, more, I learned to understand the meaning of the books I read and to enjoy them. I worked with the pretty threads I liked so much, improving quickly because I loved using the silks.

Selina was always gentle, kind and patient. I came to love her almost as much as I loved Justin: which makes what I did to her even more unforgivable! However, that was still in the future and neither of us could have guessed what would happen.

So the months passed and I was content. Soon I began to learn simple Latin, this did not please me so much, for I found Mr. Renard too solemn and I would rather have been at my sewing. But Sir Ralph was a man of culture and he insisted that his family should improve their minds. I knew now that not all gentlewomen learned to read, nor did they bother with the Latin; but Sir Ralph intended the ladies of his household to be as well versed in their studies as his son, and because his word was law we obeyed him.

I asked why Justin did not take his lessons with us, for he was still studying; but Selina explained that he worked harder than we did and that Mr. Renard spent the afternoons with him. In the mornings Justin went riding, so I did not see him as often as I could have wished. Then I discovered that if I slipped away from my companions shortly before the midday meal I might find him in the armoury, cleaning his pistol. Then — if I was good and did not plague him with questions — he let me watch him practising with his pistol or taking a fencing lesson.

He would laugh, saying: "You are a strange child, Jalinda, most girls would be scared of the noise . . . "

But I would shake my head and beg him to let me stay. He would look amused but he did not send me away, and I think he was secretly pleased to have me there. As for me, I was happier than I had been since my parents' deaths and I knew how lucky I was.

If Justin and his father had not ridden by that day I would have died in the murky waters of that pond. That I was alive was a miracle, but more than this was the way Sir Ralph had taken me into his home, not as a servant but as one of his family. To be honest I did not try very hard to understand this, I had my own ideas. Had I not planned a better life than Granny's, and was I not a witch?

If I had doubted it, then I had ample

proof now. Although I spent most of my time with Selina and Thérèse, they often went riding together in the afternoons; and, since I could not yet ride, I could not accompany them. Besides, I should not have been welcome. I had already intruded too much into their companionship, and Thérèse lost no opportunity of excluding me if she could. Therefore, since I could find no way of being with Justin, I would slip down to the kitchen and sit by the fire.

Under her stern exterior Mrs. Beeson had a kind heart and she let me come and go as I wished. I liked to sit there, listening to their gossip and sipping at a mug of the creamy milk Cook always gave me. And sitting in my corner one afternoon, I heard something which made me certain that I was a witch.

"He's dead, then," said one of the footmen.

"Dead — who's that, Tim?" asked Cook, looking up from her work. He stared pointedly at me and she frowned at him. "Don't you mind, Mistress Jalinda. She takes no notice, do you, my lovey?"

I shook my head, watching Tim curiously, waiting for him to speak.

"But it were 'im as . . . " he broke off, giving an expressive jerk of his head in my direction.

Cook paled and immediately changed the subject. But I knew what Tim meant: my enemy had died, just as I had wished he would. So then I knew that I had the power. Granny had told me so, but until this moment I had doubted it. For if I was really a witch, why had I not been able to save her? But perhaps she hadn't wanted to be saved; she was old and even witches must die some time. I wanted to live and I had been rescued: so perhaps that was enough for one small witch to achieve.

I wondered how my enemy had died, but I dare not ask, it was dangerous to speak of such things. I had learned my lesson; I should never boast of my powers again.

In time I began to make a few cures. First to ease Cook's indigestion, then for the gardener's warts, and the little chambermaid who suffered with a racking cough. I was careful to use only simple things which even Cook and Mrs. Beeson understood. And when one of the maids asked me for a love potion I said that I did not know how to make them. It was safer, and the servants accepted my cures as merely simples; speaking of my being called a witch as a wicked plot on the part of my enemy — the man who had died. But they did not know I had put a curse on him, did they?

★ ★ ★

Time passed swiftly in that house. Gradually, I lost the half-starved look I had when I first came to Hallows. I was protected, secure, and my mind was opening like the bud of a flower welcoming the soft, spring rain. I was thirsty for knowledge, and Sir Ralph was never happier than when I sat at his feet before the fire, listening to his words of wisdom. Even in the Latin I made good progress, and Mr. Renard was pleased with me. He had begun to instruct me in something else, too; for he was a priest, and his duties as a tutor were only a façade to hide his identity.

Sir Ralph had decided that I was ready to enter the faith which meant so much to him. I did not object, indeed, I tried to accept it, for already my plans had taken definite shape. I wanted to be Justin's wife and I believed it would happen. I had gained so much — why should I not have all that I desired?

So I listened to the priest, outwardly accepting his words. Father Renard was a good man, with a simple trust in God. He never doubted my sincerity, nor thought to look beneath the docile, obedient face I showed the world. And I did try. I would truly have believed if I could, but my early life had been too hard. Besides, to accept everything he taught would mean that I was damned beyond forgiveness. I was a witch, a creature of sin — and I had caused a man to die.

This god of whom Father Renard spoke would surely not forgive such a wicked person as I? And even if he would, I had to be humble and think only of others, something I found impossible. What I wanted would always come first, at least until I had learned that this was the path to sorrow and despair. Perhaps if I had tried a little harder none of the terrible tragedies need have occurred. But I was still a selfish child with much to learn.

Such was my belief in myself that as the years passed I wove my secret plans, dreaming of the time when I married Justin. I was fifteen now and beginning to show signs of the beauty that was to be mine. My thin, gawkiness had disappeared and I knew that men had started to notice me. I was rather more forward in my knowledge of adulthood than either Selina or Thérèse, due to my continuing visits to the kitchen, and my silent observation of life as they lived it there.

The servants were so used to me sitting in my corner that they often forgot I was there; and so I heard things I would not have heard in the company of Selina and Thérèse. And I knew what was going on in the house in a way they never did. I knew when one of the maids was dismissed because she had got herself with child. There was much heated argument about it. Cook and Tim thought she had been unfairly treated, but Mrs. Beeson disagreed.

"Sir Ralph is a just man," she declared, "but he will have no wantonness in his house. Sara should have waited and asked his permission to wed. I only wish I knew who the father was, I'd send him packing, too!"

I saw Tim's quickly hidden start of fear and smiled. I could have told Mrs. Beeson who was the father of Sara's child, but I kept his secret. I liked to think that I knew something the others did not. It was my old desire for power again. And, soon afterwards, I was glad I had guessed his secret.

It was a winter's afternoon, dark and gloomy, with the wind howling through the trees and the sound of the rain beating against the walls. I was hurrying to my room, having stayed overlong by the kitchen fire, when I saw Tim approaching. The passage was too narrow for two people to pass, and I thought he would stand aside, but he planted himself squarely in the middle, grinning at me. He often teased me, but today I had no time to waste on silly games.

"I would pass, if you please."

He leered at me, considering my request. "Maybe, I will — and maybe, I won't . . . " He laughed, trying to catch me.

I avoided him, stamping my foot in annoyance. "Stand aside! I am late and I must change my gown before dinner."

"My! — what a fine lady she is," he said, pressing his face close to mine so that I could smell the wine on his breath. "But I wonder what she is like beneath those pretty clothes . . . "?

I moved back sharply, guessing his intentions, but he caught a handful of my long hair, forcing me to look at him. He was breathing heavily, a strange, sick glaze in his eyes. I tried to free myself, but he moved suddenly, his body pressing me hard against the wall.

"Such soft skin," he murmured, stroking my cheek, "and those green eyes — they drive me mad . . . "

I knew he had been drinking; he would not normally dare to say such things to me. I struggled but he laughed and held me all the tighter. "Please, Tim, release me," I said. "Don't be foolish."

"A fool? Perhaps I am, but I can't help it. Love me, Jalinda," he begged. "Let me come to your room — I'll show you who you really are, beneath those prissy manners . . . "

My eyes blazed with anger. "I am not Sara!" I spat the words at him. "If you touch me again, you'll be sorry. I'm warning you! I'll have you dismissed and whipped until your back is raw."

He jerked back as though he had been stung; his face paled and his mouth went slack. He released me and I wriggled past him, running off down the passage. Reaching the end, I stopped and looked back. He was still staring after me.

"It's all right, Tim." I called softly. "I won't tell — but remember I could . . . " I laughed and darted up the stairs.

He never again tried to touch me, though I would see his eyes followed me wherever I went; and it pleased me to know that he was a little afraid of me.

★ ★ ★

A few weeks after this incident another link was forged in the chain of my destiny, though I thought it unimportant at the time. It did not concern me, so it did not interest me.

We were to have visitors; two young men, second cousins of Justin's mother. She had been a Frenchwoman, and the cousins, like Justin and Thérèse, were half French, half English. They had lived mostly in France so it was the cause of great excitement that they were coming to Hallows. And there was a special reason for their journey.

Thérèse was nearly sixteen and she was to be betrothed to one of her cousins. They were named Stefan and Geraint Fontaine; and it was to the younger, Stefan, that she was promised. Her excitement and pleasure even extended to me as she told me her news.

"We shall be betrothed in the chapel," she said, smiling confidently. "And then in a few months we shall be married; first in the village church and then secretly in the chapel. Stefan is a Catholic, too, of course — that is why it has been arranged so long; there are so few with whom we could marry."

I looked at her, puzzled. She had said 'We' — what did she mean? I was soon answered.

"I shall be married before Justin," she went on. "It is different for a man. He will go into the King's service for a year and marry Selina when he returns."

I stared at her, my mind whirling from the shock. Justin and Selina were promised to each other! How could that be? Thérèse saw my dismay and despite her happiness, she still hated me enough to enjoy telling me what she guessed would hurt me.

"Of course — didn't you know?" she asked, looking sly. "They have been betrothed for years. Selina's father is a cousin of ours, and he is always beside the King — so she came to live with us when her mother died."

She watched eagerly, hoping to see

my pain, but it was well hidden. I had my feelings under control now. "That explains it," I said airily, as if it was of no importance to me — no importance! — when all my nerves were screaming and my brain felt as if it were on fire.

Thérèse was surprised and I realised she must have guessed at least a part of my love for Justin. But after staring at my expressionless face for a while, she shrugged and began to talk of her betrothal again.

I smiled, answering in all the right places, but inside I was writhing in torment. Justin and Selina! Impossible — he was mine! My whole being cried out that he belonged to me and I knew I could not let her have him. She was not right for him: he needed someone brighter and quicker — me. We were meant for each other; and I had seen a certain look in his eyes which betrayed him. He wanted me as much as I wanted him.

They were betrothed and a betrothal

was almost as scared as the marriage vow itself, but I would not let that stand in my way. I should not meekly bow my head and watch him wed Selina. He was and must be mine!

I did not know how I should prevent their marriage; I just knew that I would do it somehow. If I felt guilty about Selina, who had been so good to me, then I brushed the thought aside. I was naturally sorry to hurt her, but she did not love Justin as I did.

She might be angry at first, but then she would find someone else. I began to try to think of a way to bind Justin to me, so firmly that he would not escape, or want to escape a life with me as his wife. I convinced myself that it was for his happiness as much as mine. Selina would be hurt but it was better for one to suffer than two. Besides, it was what I wanted and that was what really mattered, of course!

★ ★ ★

The cousins came and at first I took little notice of them, or they of me. Stefan had eyes for no one but Thérèse; in any case he did not interest me. I thought him dull and rather foolish. I looked at my Justin, thinking how plain he made his cousins appear. Although I allowed the elder brother to be handsome in a dark, forbidding way. He wore his brown hair long, his eyes were grey and his skin had a sunburned look. I preferred the fairness of Justin's skin, but then, anyone would show to disadvantage beside my Justin.

I still thought of him as mine, though I had not yet found the way to make certain of this, but I had plenty of time. Justin was to spend a year at court before his wedding. However, I intended to return there as his bride instead of Selina. But if I could, I would find a way which did not hurt her too much; for I was fond of her.

At the start, the cousins' visit made little difference to me — except that I should be glad when they left. Justin spent all his time with them, so I saw him less than usual.

Geraint was already at court and travelled widely in the King's service. The younger men admired him and even Sir Ralph listened when he spoke. At night they would sit before the fire, discussing matters of state. The men hung on his words, while both Selina and Thérèse seemed interested in what he had to say; but I was bored with all this grave talk of dissent between the King and his Parliament, and I wished he would tell us about the latest fashions instead.

One evening he noticed my bored stare and I saw a flash of amusement in his eyes. He smiled at me, arousing my interest momentarily. I smiled back, lowering my eyes modestly as I had seen Selina do sometimes. Perhaps I did not do it in quite the right way, for he looked even more amused, almost as if he could see through to the true feelings beneath my modesty.

"Enough of this for one evening,"

he said. "I am sure the ladies would prefer news of the court and the latest fashions. Stefan, you are better at describing them than I — tell our fair companions what they would like to hear."

"Willingly, brother," replied Stefan.

I sat forward eagerly as he began, agog to hear the scandals of the court, and whether hair was to be shorter or longer, and what were the latest fal-lals of the fashionable ladies. I was so interested in Stefan's description of some new lace and a way of tying the band-strings that I did not immediately notice the look on Geraint's face.

He was highly diverted and, as his eyes met mine, he winked at me. I tossed my head, sitting back and pretending to lose interest. But my action only served to make him laugh, and after a while my curiosity forced me to ask Stefan about one of the new stuffs. I struggled not to look in Geraint's direction, but, of course, in the end I did, and that hateful smile was still on his face. I scowled at him. How dare he make fun of me?!

The next morning he sought me out in the garden and began a conversation. I answered him as shortly as I could, but he ignored my churlishness, talking of things he knew would interest me. My attention was caught, albeit unwillingly, and I asked him questions about his life at court. We spent a pleasant half hour together, and I had come to think him a reasonable companion after all, when he suddenly asked me a question which threw me off my guard.

"And when are you to be betrothed?" he said, smiling at me.

I stared at him foolishly. "Betrothed?" I echoed. "I am not going to be betrothed . . . "

"No?" He was polite enough, but something in his voice and the way he smiled irked me. "Then perhaps you will be surprised one day . . . "

"What do you mean?"

"Why nothing, mistress — except

that I am sure your guardian will arrange something for you. Mayhap next year, when you are sixteen."

"I shall choose my own husband!" I snapped, meeting his eyes defiantly.

"Why, so I hope, Jalinda, but it will have to meet with Sir Ralph's approval, you know. Let us hope that you may both be satisfied. I sincerely wish it to be that way."

He looked at me oddly and I felt a stab of fear. Something in his expression frightened me. I believed he was telling me that he knew of such an arrangement, and I thought it probable that Sir Ralph had asked his advice; for I knew he respected this young man. I was gripped with a wild panic: time was shorter than I had believed! I tried to make Geraint tell me more, but he only smiled in that maddening way and said that I must be patient. I grew angry with him again, and as Thérèse and Stefan approached, I left him to their company.

The next day the cousins departed;

and though Geraint smiled at me and kissed my hand, I gave him no more than a cold "God-speed". He seemed disappointed, even hurt and I was glad. He had grossly offended me.

★ ★ ★

As soon as the cousins had gone I hastily formed my plans. Selina's feelings were no longer sufficiently important to risk further delay. In three weeks Justin would leave too, and I had to bind him to me, so that when he thought of me it would be with desire and not as his little sister.

I had never learned to ride, though he had often tried to persuade me, but I was secretly afraid of the great, snorting beasts. Now, however, there was no time for dallying: I had to find a way of being alone with Justin and I would risk anything if it brought me closer to my heart's desire.

I begged Justin to teach me to ride. He looked at me in amazement as well he might when I had always avoided the subject. But I explained earnestly that I felt it my duty to overcome my fear. "If you were to teach me, Justin," I said, looking innocent. "I think I could face it."

"Certainly Justin will teach you, Jalinda," Selina insisted, with a warm smile for me. "I have often thought you ought to be able to ride — and you will be quite safe with Justin, my dear."

She smiled at both of us and I felt a pang of guilt. How strange that she should help me to steal her betrothed from her; but, of course, she was just being kind as usual. She would never suspect the wickedness in my heart.

So our lessons began. I lost no chance to take full advantage of our time together, seeming to know instinctively what to do. I had to be helped to and from the saddle, and I made certain that it was Justin who put his hands about my waist to lift me on to my horse's back. I had to be shown how to hold the reins, and I managed to brush my hands lightly against his. For someone who learns quickly, it was surprising how often I needed to be shown what I must do!

I smiled and sighed, looking helpless and fragile. And I could see quite plainly the effect it was having on Justin, though he tried hard to fight his desire for me. But I knew my body had begun to show the promise of the curves it would one day have in abundance and I knew that I had something else as well. It was an indefinable quality which I did not understand, but it made men look at me with hot, lustful eyes. I had seen the look in Tim's face and now it was in Justin's, too. He no longer thought of me as a little girl.

I was content with that, but the imp of fate decided to help me.

We were out riding, and though I pretended otherwise, I was beginning to ride well. Seized with a desire to put my skill to the test, I called to

Justin to follow, urging my horse to a gallop. He laughed, digging his heels in sharply and giving chase. We raced for a while and the groom was soon left far behind as our fine thoroughbreds sped on ahead.

All at once a fox appeared from nowhere, running straight across my path. I tugged frantically at the reins, and my horse stopped abruptly, rearing up in fright. I was thrown to the ground and lay still, winded by the fall. Justin leapt to the ground and hurried to my side. I believe he thought I was dead and his fear lent itself to my aid.

"Jalinda — my beloved!" he cried.

As I stirred and held out my arms to him, he swept me up in a passionate embrace. The next moment his lips were on mine and he was kissing me fiercely. I clung to him, responding with all my heart. He held me for a long moment, then drew away, a queer, blind look in his eyes.

"I am sorry," he said. "I should not have done that."

"But why?" I cried. "I love you and you love me — what is wrong with confessing it?"

He looked grave as he helped me to my feet and stood with his arms about me. "I am betrothed to Selina," he said. "It is almost like being married. You could not know, Jalinda — but I did and I am entirely to blame."

"But you do not love her, Justin — you love me!" I cried, tears in my eyes.

"Yes, I do — and I think I always shall love you. But it is a matter of honour. I cannot break my word to her — and if I would, my father would forbid it."

"Then you will marry her and break my heart?"

He stared at me and his eyes were filled with pain. "I don't know, Jalinda — I don't know . . . " His voice broke despairingly. "How can I break my word?"

I looked at him fearfully, was I to lose him despite all my scheming? It could not be! I would find a way somehow. But for now it must be enough that Justin had discovered he loved and wanted me. Tomorrow he was to leave for the King's army, and now he would carry his longing with him. A year was a long time and he might come to realise that it was foolish to resist this feeling between us. If not, then there were other ways . . . Was I not a witch and had I not the power? If need be, I would use it. I would make Justin break his tryst with Selina and I would sweep all opposition from my path. As we rode back to Hallows I silently vowed that he should never marry anyone but me . . .

3

IT seemed that fate was determined to help me. Justin had been in the King's service for only seven months when Sir Ralph fell ill. It was very sudden. One day he was well, the next he was seized by a mysterious sickness which took the power from his legs, confining him to his bed. I was saddened to see him brought so low, and I did not at first realise that this was to be the means by which I would gain my heart's desire.

Sir Ralph had always treated me kindly and I knew how much I owed him. My life, my home, the very clothes I wore were all his gift to me. I had never understood why he had taken me into his home and raised me as a member of his family. I merely admired him for his generosity and now that he was ill, I did all I could to please him.

I sat for hours, reading to him, or talking of the pictures he loved so much. It was a quiet period in my life, and one in which I genuinely thought of someone besides myself. For a time I even ceased to dream of Justin.

At first we thought Sir Ralph would recover, but then he had another seizure which left his face twisted on one side. After this, Selina and I were his only companions, for Thérèse could not bear to look at him and he would see none of his old friends. He drew closer to me, wanting me always at his side and never happy unless I was in his room. I was pleased to be of service to him, and spent most of my days at his bedside. But he grew weaker and we decided that Justin must be sent for.

I swear I did not plan it so, my thoughts were only of Sir Ralph. It was Selina who suggested that Justin should come home, and I agreed. But I will not deny that my heart beat faster at the thought of his return. However, I had no schemes to turn my guardian's illness to my advantage. Nor did I plan what happened next — though I could have prevented it. But perhaps that would have been asking too much of me.

Justin came home. I shall never forget the look of pain on his face that day, nor how much I longed to take him in my arms and comfort him. But I could only stand and watch as Selina went to greet him, leading him into his father's room. We sat together by Sir Ralph's bed; Justin, Selina and I. We were so close then that the love between us was a tangible thing.

I was tired. I had kept a vigil by Sir Ralph for the past five nights and I intended to sit with him again; but Selina saw my weariness.

"You must rest, Jalinda," she said. "Let me take your place tonight."

I shook my head, protesting that I was not tired. She looked concerned and I know she was about to insist when Justin intervened.

"You both need rest. I will keep watch myself."

Selina and I exchanged glances, silently agreeing: it was natural that Justin should want to be with his father. We said goodnight and left them to go to our beds, for we were both weary. However, I had not slept for very long before I was roughly awakened by someone shaking me.

"Come quickly, Mistress Jalinda!"

It was Mrs. Beeson, her face pale in the candlelight.

I jumped out of bed, throwing a wrap over my night-chemise. My heart was thumping painfully as I hurried to Sir Ralph's room. Entering, I could see that he was having some kind of a fit, choking and threshing wildly while Justin tried vainly to calm him. He looked at me helplessly, crying:

"Jalinda — what can I do?!"

I sent Mrs. Beeson scurrying to fetch a mixture I had prepared earlier. She was gone for only a few moments, but as we watched the sick man's convulsions it seemed an eternity. When she returned, I poured the liquid into a cup and held it to Sir Ralph's lips, but it just ran away from his clenched teeth.

"Force his mouth open, Justin!"

Justin stared at me stupidly. He was bewildered, unable to move. I frowned at him, but even as he hesitated, Selina came in and saw the situation at a glance. She prised Sir Ralph's mouth open long enough for me to pour some of the mixture down his throat. It was a while before it took effect, but gradually his wild threshing quietened and then he slept.

"Go back to bed, Jalinda, you look exhausted," said Selina. "I will stay here, my dear."

"Very well," I replied. "I believe he will sleep until morning now."

I smiled at her and went back to my room. To my surprise, Justin came with me. He seemed ill at ease and when I reached my bedchamber, he followed me inside. A protest rose to my lips:

he should not be here with me! Then I looked at his face and it died unspoken. His eyes were dark pools of misery; and, slumping in a chair, he covered his face with his hands and wept.

"I thought he was going to die — I couldn't move. I don't want him to die . . . "

Love and pity welled up in me like a great tide. I longed to ease his pain and I knelt beside him, holding his head against me and stroking that soft, fair hair. I only thought to comfort him, but he trembled violently, as if shaken by a storm of feeling. Suddenly, he swept me up in his arms and, in one swift movement, he carried me to the bed. I did not resist as he lay down beside me and I let him remove my night-chemise. I lay still, thrilling to the touch of his hands and glorying in the passionate kisses which covered my body.

"Oh, my love," he whispered. "How I have longed to hold you like this, to touch your beautiful body and kiss your sweet lips. Forgive me, Jalinda — I have tried to put you out of my mind, but you are a part of me. I cannot live without you."

"Justin, Justin, I love you. I love you," I sobbed, tears of joy running down my cheeks.

He drew me to him then and I clung to him in ecstasy as our bodies and thoughts merged into one and I was his. It was wonderful, exciting, all I had dreamed of and more. At last I knew what it meant to be a woman, and I knew what it was about me that turned men's heads. I was made for love, and for the pleasure which comes only between a man and a woman.

I do not believe that Justin was really aware of what he did; his grief and his longing for me had overcome his sense of honour. He needed my love, and the comfort of my body. I gave it to him and he did not think beyond that — but I did. At last I had what I wanted. He would have to break his promise to Selina now. In his code he had dishonoured me and he would do what was right. I smiled as I lay beside him in the darkness. Now I knew that he was mine!

If Justin had spoken to his father our lives might have been very different, though much of the harm was already done. But perhaps I alone would have suffered and that was only just — for I was most to blame.

Sir Ralph improved after that night and we began to hope for his eventual recovery, but it was very slow. For two months Justin stayed at home, fearing to leave lest his father worsened. In that time we were lovers as often as possible, and I knew his father was not the only reason he lingered at Hallows.

I kept asking him when he would speak to his father of our marriage, but he always made some excuse. The time was not right; his father was not so well, he was waiting for a suitable moment. I knew we must consider Sir Ralph's health; it was bound to be a shock to him, and it could not hurt to wait for a while. But at the end of two months I knew we could delay no more. I was with child and I told Justin so.

"Are you sure?" he asked, looking alarmed. "Surely it is too soon to know?"

"There is no doubt, Justin."

I made him promise to speak to his father that same night, but morning came and still he had not spoken. I knew then what I had long suspected: Justin was afraid to tell his father. I would have to tell him myself.

Was I too impatient? Should I have waited or would the shock always have been too much for him? If only I had been patient — but that is pointless. If I had been dutiful; if I had sent Justin away; if I had died of the pox . . . If, if, if! How many times in future years was I to ask myself these questions? But the answer was always the same. I wish that I had waited, but I had always been quick to act on my decisions.

The next day I went to Sir Ralph's room. He was pleased to see me; I had spent less of my time with him since Justin's return. When I saw how tenderly he smiled at me, my courage almost deserted me. I knew that what I had to say would hurt and shame him and I was filled with remorse. I talked for a while of unimportant things, fussing round the bed in a manner so unlike my normal self that he sensed something was wrong.

"What is it, Jalinda?" he asked, regarding me anxiously. "There is trouble in your heart, I can feel it. Will you not tell me what ails you? I have never told you how dear you are to me, but you must know that I care for you deeply. Come — unburden your heart to me."

Tears trembled on my lashes. I blinked them back: it was now or never. "Justin and I want to be wed. I know it is wrong — that Selina will be hurt — but we are in love . . . " I ended on a note of defiance as I saw his face.

He looked stricken. "No, Jalinda, you can't — it is impossible!"

I stared at him sullenly. He had refused without even thinking of how we felt. It was easy for him to say he cared for me — but how could he refuse me if that was true?

"But why?" I asked, my voice petulant. "I know Justin is betrothed to Selina, but a betrothal can be broken."

"No, Jalinda. A marriage between you and Justin is out of the question. No, I say!" His hands shook and there was a queer look in his eyes. "It is impossible . . ."

He was evidently in great distress, but I was past caring for anything but my own selfish desires. "It has to be broken!" I cried without thinking. "I am with child and Justin is the father of my child . . ."

I broke off as I saw him recoil in horror. He sared at me, disbelief and sorrow mingling with the pain. I was frightened I had not meant to tell

105

him that part of my story unless it was vital.

"With child," he echoed hoarsely. "Justin — my son. You and Justin — but you can't. It is wrong, evil. God! — how I am punished for my sins! I should have told you . . . "

He got no further. His face turned purple, his eyes rolled upwards and he began to choke. At once I forgot our quarrel; I forgot Justin and our guilty love-affair. I went to him, loosening the neck of his nightgown and holding a cup of water to his lips; but his face was rigid, his teeth clenched so that the water ran down his chin. I ran to the door, screaming for help. When I returned to the bed he was mouthing something and pointing at me desperately, but I could not understand him. I thought he wanted my rosary and so I took off the chaplet he had given me, putting it into his hands. He shook his head, but after a moment he began to pull the beads through his fingers and they seemed to comfort him. I saw a tear run down his cheek and I was smitten with remorse.

"I am sorry — so very sorry," I whispered.

He was no longer gasping for air, but his eyes were dull and his breathing was laboured. Watching the colour drain from his cheeks, I wept silently. This man who had given me so much was dying, and I had caused his death. Then Justin and Selina came, and behind them, Father Renard. It was clear to everyone that Sir Ralph was dying and the priest began to say the last prayers.

I watched in a terrible agony of mind and soul as his breath came ever more slowly; then, when I could bear it no more, he breathed his last. The rosary slipped from his hands and Father Renard picked it up. He closed the staring eyes, then he brought the chaplet to me, pressing it into my hands.

"That was well done of you, mistress," he said.

I looked up into his quiet face and I could bear my guilt no longer. I fell to my knees before him, weeping bitterly.

"It was my fault!" I cried. "I should not have let it happen. I should not have let it happen . . . "

He misunderstood me. They all misunderstood, and they all tried to comfort me.

"Nay, there was nothing you could have done to prevent it — it was God's will," he said.

I shook my head. I wanted to tell them all that I had killed him by my wickedness, but I could not speak.

"It was not your fault, Jalinda," said Justin. "If it were not for you he would have died weeks ago. You and Selina did all you could. It was no one's fault."

Looking up, I saw the pain in his eyes, and I knew that I would never be able to confess my guilt; for was it not partly Justin's too? I was glad then that I had been the one to tell Sir Ralph, if he had to be told, because I knew I was stronger than Justin. He would have been for ever haunted, while I would learn to live with my guilt in time. I must bear it alone; this must be my punishment. I let them lead me away, still weeping, knowing that nothing could ever wash away my sin. I had killed a man who had shown me only kindness, and I should never forget it.

* * *

We waited until after Sir Ralph was buried, then we told Selina that Justin would marry me. We told her together, because he could not face her alone.

She listened in silence, and only the look in her eyes showed how deeply she was hurt. I had been wrong to imagine that her love for Justin was not as strong as mine. Her gentle, patient manner had deceived me; and why should she not have been serene? She had believed herself safe in Justin's care. She stared at us with her soft, wounded eyes, and not until I told her that I was with child did she speak.

"You poor child," she said, looking angrily at Justin. "Did you have to shame Jalinda as well as me?"

"It was my fault, Selina!" I cried.

But she would not have it so. She shook her head, her eyes reproachful as she said: "Justin knew that I would have released him if he had asked." She was deathly pale, trembling.

"I am glad Sir Ralph never knew — he would have been ashamed of you, Justin. Jalinda is still a child and under your protection. It is clearly your duty to marry her. I ask only one thing of you — that you delay the wedding until after my father comes to fetch me."

Justin nodded, silent and ashamed. But not so ashamed as I.

"Where will you go?" I asked. "This is your home . . . "

"I shall go to France and enter a convent."

I stared at her, horrified. "You can't

spend the rest of your life shut away from the world," I cried. "You are young — you will find someone else . . . "

She shook her head. "No. I will take no one else, Jalinda. In my heart I am Justin's wife and my faith will allow me only one husband. Since I cannot have him — then I shall give my life to the service of God. Now — I would be alone."

I could not believe it. I had been so certain that she would not mind so very much, even persuading myself that she would be happy to choose her husband herself. But I had wanted to believe that, hadn't I? I saw she would not be swayed, and I flinched at the pain in her eyes. I knew that Selina was no more suited to a life in a convent than I. True, she was gentle and good whereas I was selfish and thoughtless, but she was born to have children and a home. I had robbed her of these things and her unhappiness would weigh heavily on me.

If she had been angry it might have been easier to bear, but she did not blame us for our love. She was disappointed in Justin, but only because she thought he had wronged me, whom she loved. And I loved her. I realised too late how much I cared for this gentle girl who had done so much for me. Tears started to my eyes. Selina came to me then, putting her arms about me, she tried to comfort me. It was too much! I broke from her arms and fled.

In the following weeks I did not see her again. I could not face the girl I had wronged. I watched from an upper window as her father took her away. I saw the anger on his face, but Selina glanced up, smiling at me in her old sweet way. Why could she not have hated me? I could have borne her hatred so much easier than her love.

So now I had destroyed three people I loved: Granny, Sir Ralph and Selina. How much more trouble would I wreak before I came to know myself? I began to think my enemy had spoken truly all those years ago; for I had brought nothing but grief to this house.

★ ★ ★

Three days after Selina left, Justin and I were married. First in the village church and then, secretly, in the chapel at Hallows. Father Renard looked at me sadly, but it was Justin who received his censure. Poor Justin. He was blamed by everyone, except Thérèse and I. I knew the truth and I think Thérèse had her suspicions.

She was angry because I was to marry Justin instead of Selina, but she was careful not to show it too plainly, for I was mistress of Hallows now and her wedding was not yet arranged. She did not wish for an open quarrel while we must remain beneath the same roof.

Justin wrote to Stefan, telling him of Sir Ralph's death and arranging the wedding for three months' time.

It could not be earlier because Thérèse was in mourning for her father, indeed it was soon enough. But the trouble between the King and his Parliament was becoming increasingly serious, so much so that even I was forced to listen to the rumours of a war. So Thérèse's marriage would be in three months' time and mine at once.

I could not wait unless I wished to show my shame to the world; and Justin was very conscious of what people would think. We decided to tell the curious that our wedding had been planned before Sir Ralph's death and that he had expressed a wish for it to go ahead. Since Justin's betrothal was not known outside the family, most would believe us. There would be some gossip, but not as much as there would be if we waited until my condition became apparent.

So we were married and though I guessed that Thérèse was angry, it was not from her that the main opposition came. Surprisingly, Mrs.

Beeson showed her disapproval plainly. I had thought her my friend, but when I told her my news she looked shocked.

"But you cannot, Mistress Jalinda," she said. "'Twud not be right."

"How dare you?" I demanded. "Remember who you are and who I am . . . "

"That's the trouble, mistress," she muttered, looking strange. "I am not sure who you are. If I was sure — but I've no proof . . . "

What was she talking about? She knew very well who I was; it was simply her spite. She could not bear to see me the mistress of Hallows!

"I do not know what you mean." I glared at her. "But you had best watch your tongue if you want to keep your place here!"

She looked alarmed. She realised that it was no idle threat and she had no wish to look for a new situation. She said no more, merely grumbling to herself and eyeing me queerly. I ignored her. She would learn to accept me in time. If not — then she would have to go: it was quite simple.

But Mrs. Beeson knew her station, and she never mentioned the subject again. On my wedding morning she brought me my bride-clothes and a bride-lace tied with rosemary to bind around the sleeves of my gown. There had been no time for me to gather a trousseau, but what were new clothes to me when I was to have my heart's desire?

With Selina gone from the house, I was able to push my guilt to a secret corner of my heart, where it would lie unheeded until something brought it to mind, and shamed me again. But my own happiness had always been my first concern and so it was now. I had Justin and he loved me. He was besotted with his new wife and never tired of telling me so. I was content and when he asked me if I was happy, I replied with truth:

"Happier than I have even been, my love."

He laughed and kissed me, whispering my name as he held me close. Then I had no time to think of things which might have robbed me of my joy.

Soon we were to go to London and the court. The King was quarrelling with Parliament, which was no new thing, but this time it seemed more serious. Because the King felt a need to gather his supporters about him, we were summoned urgently. Justin was to be a captain in the cavalry, and I was to be presented to Their Majesties. It seemed that I could ask no more of life, my dreams had all come true. I prepared for the journey to London in a fever of excitement.

★ ★ ★

The life at court was all that I had ever imagined. Perhaps because of my childhood when I had known hunger and privation I took an excessive delight in the splendours of the palace and the gaiety I found there, for though there was unrest in the kingdom it did not yet affect the life at court. We danced, sang, feasted and generally made merry, as though everything was just as it ought to be. Indeed, to us, it was, for none of us really believed that Parliament would dare to take up arms against the King. Surely they would stop short of treason!

Justin and his friends laughed as they sat drinking in the evenings, and they all agreed that if those sour-faced, righteous men were foolish enough to turn against their King — who ruled by divine right and had been crowned absolute monarch of this land — then it would be the worse for them; for how could an unruly, untrained rabble hope to stand against the King's men? And all men of right thinking must rally to his standard, for whatever their views on his policies, they would not risk opposing him by force of arms. So it must all come to nothing in the end, and, once tempers had cooled, this talk of war would be forgotten.

As for me, I was spoiled and fêted as Justin's bride; and his friends fell over themselves to dance with me, bring me nosegays, and write sonnets to my eyes. I was never alone, never dull, and if I needed an escort, there was a surfeit of gallants to walk beside my sedan chair as I was carried about the city. Indeed, I was so popular that Justin was a little jealous of his friends; but only a little, for he knew that I was truly his, and I believe he was happy in those short weeks we spent at court. I pray that it was so, for we were to have scant joy in the future.

For three months I lived in a whirl of pleasure. Thérèse had accompanied us to buy her bride-clothes; and I went with her to all the silk merchants, purchasing as many new gowns as I desired. Justin lavished gifts on me, and if I did not buy the trinkets which caught my eyes, then he bought them for me. He gave me a caul of gold and pearls, worked in a trellis pattern; precious silks, velvets, laces, and an emerald necklace which he said matched the colour of my eyes.

He took me everywhere, proud of his wife whom he thought so wonderful. One afternoon we went to the theatre. He would not take me in the evening for too many playhouses had burned down because they used pitch flares to light the gloom — and Justin would not risk his precious wife in such a cause!

I did not care for the theatre much, though I had plagued him to take me there. It was hot, stuffy, the air thick with the blue smoke of tobacco. Besides, it was difficult to hear the players above the noise of the audience. They called ribald greetings to one another, constantly moving about as if they had come more to show off their fine clothes than to watch the play. I had particularly wanted to see this play, *The Merchant of Venice*, but as Portia reached her immortal speech, saying: "The quality of mercy is not strained it . . . " — a voice from the audience called out:

"Show me a little mercy, Portia, and warm my bed tonight!"

This sally was greeted with raucous laughter and similar suggestions. Portia — who turned out to be a fair-faced youth — came to the front of the stage, offering to oblige the speaker in a manner which brought a flush to my cheeks. The crowd cheered, delighted by this speech which owed nothing to Will Shakespeare; but for me the play was spoilt. I asked Justin to take me away and I did not pester him to go there again; instead, we had amateur theatricals with our friends. We even performed a masque before the King and Queen, and His Majesty congratulated us on our performance.

It was said that he was a cold man but I never found him so, nor did I see the intolerance of which his ministers complained so bitterly. I thought him charming, gracious and kind. I liked the Queen less, but perhaps that was because she was a woman and rather proud. I preferred men, and they liked me. With the ladies of the court I was unpopular, but this did not bother me; I had never needed the approval of other women. Besides, I was far too happy to concern myself with their sly glances or malicious whispers. I wished that I could remain at the palace for ever, but I knew that this was not possible.

We were returning to Hallows shortly, to prepare for Thérèse's wedding. It would be months before I could come back. Justin had discreetly mentioned that I was increasing, and I should not be expected until after the child was weaned, though no one guessed how soon my child would be born.

I had laced myself tightly and I wore a busk to hide my swelling waist. Myself, I cared not if people guessed the truth, and I did not believe our friends would care either. But Justin was adamant, lest gossip came to the Queen's ears and she refused to accept me as one of her ladies-in-waiting. I shuddered at the thought of being excluded from that merry life and forced to remain at Hallows, alone. So I laced myself even tighter, to hide just how far gone with child I really was.

★ ★ ★

Justin helped me into the coach, placing a coverlet over my gown and tucking it around my long, silk buskins to keep my legs warm; for there was a chill in the autumn air and we had a long way to travel.

"Are you warm enough?" he asked.

"Yes, thank you." I laughed at his anxious face.

"Are you comfortable — have you everything you need?"

"My maid will look to my comfort. Do not fuss so much, my love."

"But it is a long journey and you are five months . . . " He broke off, looking conscious as Thérèse stared at him.

"I am well enough," I said, pulling a face at him.

He laughed, closed the carriage door

and mounted his horse as we moved off. Thérèse was looking at me and I realised that his mistake had been duly noted by her. Once she would have smiled at me in her superior way, now she seemed different, quieter, even anxious. I was soon to discover why.

Her mother had died when she was born and she knew nothing of the realities of married life, simply because there had been no one to tell her. Her father had spoken of Stefan's suitability, and Father Renard of her duty to marry a Catholic, but they had not told her what her duties to her husband would be. She vaguely expected to bear children, but she knew nothing of how those children came into being. She asked me shyly what it was like to be married and I told her frankly what she wanted to know. Poor girl, I think it was a shock to her. I was glad that I had spent half my childhood in the kitchens — but then, I was born with the knowledge in me. To me the act of love was instinctive, as natural as the air I breathed. I had not realised it was not so with every woman, indeed, that it could cause repulsion and even fear.

"Do — do you like being married?" she asked.

I smiled at her. "Yes, I like being married, because I love Justin."

"I — I am not sure if I will . . . " she confessed, blushing and staring down at her lap as she twisted her gloves nervously.

"Of course you will. You love Stefan, don't you?"

"I think so . . . " she faltered and could not go on.

"You must not be frightened, Thérèse," I said, trying to comfort her. "It will be all right, you'll see."

She tossed her head indignantly. "I'm not afraid," she snapped, turning away. For a while we travelled in silence; however, she needed to talk and soon she began again: "It was different for you. You fell in love with Justin and you have known him for years. I had only met Stefan once before we were betrothed, when we were children . . . "

I studied her face. She was fine-boned and delicate and her mouth had a sulky droop at the corners. I felt sorry for her and squeezed her hand. "Are you unhappy?" I asked. "Because if you are I will speak to Justin. You need not marry Stefan if you don't want to. We can have the betrothal broken . . . " She looked horrified. "Break my word to Stefan? Go against my father's wishes? It would be wicked — I wonder that you can suggest it!"

I shrugged and said no more. It was her choice, but I knew I would never have married a man I did not love just because it had been arranged.

How fate must have smiled that day, knowing what was in store for me. One day I should look back and wonder at my innocence. I little understood my own nature, even though I thought myself so clever!

4

WE had been at Hallows a week when Stefan arrived. He came alone, explaining that his brother was in France on King Charles's business.

"Geraint sends his love and bade me tell you that he will be here in two days, Jalinda," he said, smiling at me as if he thought I should be anxious for such news.

I stared at him, puzzled by his manner. "We wondered why Geraint was not at court," I said, "but if he was in France that explains it."

Stefan was silent, looking from me to Justin. Suddenly he realised that I was Justin's wife and he looked surprised, almost offended. Obviously he had not known of our marriage until this moment; and as I turned to Justin I saw a guilty expression on his face. I had thought he would tell his cousins of our nuptials in his letter, but it seemed that he had not. I understand his reason: he had been ashamed to tell them because they knew of his betrothal to Selina, and Justin would always put off an unpleasant duty if he could.

* * *

I was alone in the garden, picking flowers when Geraint arrived. He came upon me by surprise, a look of delight on his darkly handsome face. Turning to see him watching me, I found that my heart was beating wildly, bringing a flush to my cheeks. He saw the welcome in my eyes and held out his hands to me.

"Jalinda! You are pleased to see me — so Sir Ralph told you . . . "

"Told me what, Geraint?" I asked, smiling at him. "What should he have told me?"

I was puzzled both by his manner

and the way my heart was behaving. Naturally I was pleased to see him; he was my husband's favourite cousin, but I had not felt the same joy at seeing Stefan. Gazing up at him in bewilderment, I realised that his smile was that of a lover.

He laughed. "Sir Ralph may not have told you — but surely you guessed?"

"Guessed what, Geraint?" I asked, impatient now.

"Of our betrothal. It was arranged when I was here last year. Sir Ralph agreed that we should be betrothed after Thérèse's wedding. You must have known what I was hinting at that day?"

I gasped. How foolish I had been not to understand that he was telling me he had offered for me! Looking up into his dark eyes, I had a brief pang of regret, a feeling of irreplaceable loss, as though I had missed something wonderful. I thrust it away quickly. I had no right to feel like that: I was married to Justin. It was the fulfilment of my dreams. I did not really know this man who was making my pulses race, and from whom I had parted with dislike a few months ago. He frowned, waiting for my answer; and I flushed, conscious of my thickening waist.

"I am sorry, Geraint. Sir Ralph told me nothing of this, and now it is too late — I am Justin's wife."

He gave a start and I saw the dawning horror in his eyes; just as I had seen it in Sir Ralph's when I told him I was carrying his son's child. A cold hand gripped my heart and I felt that something was terribly wrong.

"I know it must be a shock," I said, playing for time. I did not want to know why he was looking at me like that. "But we were not betrothed so — so it has not harmed you . . . " I faltered, my mouth dry with fear.

"Harmed me?" he echoed. "That is not important — though it is not true — but it is what it has done to you, and Justin, that matters." He paused, his face contorting with pain; then he squared his shoulders as though a great burden had been placed upon them. "You will have to leave Justin immediately after the wedding. I shall take you to my mother in France. She will care for you until we can have the marriage dissolved — somehow! — and then I shall marry you. Do not be afraid, Jalinda, I shall protect you — and I swear before God that I will never reproach you for what has happened."

The fear was almost suffocating me as I looked up at him. "Leave Justin — go with you? I do not understand you . . . " I did not want to understand!

"You cannot stay with Justin — it is a sin against God and man. You have no choice, Jalinda."

"For pity's sake, tell me what you mean!" I cried; but in my heart I had begun to suspect the horrible truth.

"Did you never wonder why Sir Ralph raised you as his own — can it be that you have no idea of who you are? Of course, it must be so . . . "

The blood drained from my face and the world span crazily. I gasped, shaking my head at him. "No! Please, no! You do not mean it, you cannot . . . " Suddenly I beat at his chest, shouting that he was lying, screaming hysterically as my whole world collapsed in ruins. Geraint slapped my face sharply, taking me in his arms as I slumped against him.

"You are his daughter, Jalinda," he said, stroking my hair as I wept on his shoulder. "Justin is your half-brother. You have no choice — think what might happen if . . . " He broke off with a new horror in his eyes.

"It is too late," I whispered, the sickness rising in my throat. "I am already carrying Justin's child . . . "

"God forgive me!" he cried. "I should have prevented this."

I stared at him with dull eyes, knowing only too well who was to blame. I was a cheat, a murderess, and guilty of yet another deadly sin. But it was my father's death which tormented me; Sir Ralph, my father! He had not been able to bear the terrible thing I had blurted out so thoughtlessly. My own mind reeled from the horror of it, and I clung to my sanity by searching my memory for a clue — anything — which might have revealed the truth to me long ago.

But I had believed that kindly man, who died when I was eight years old, my father. How could I have guessed otherwise when he had never given a sign that I was not his child? But it explained so many things which had puzzled me. I understood why my mother had run away — and why Granny was so angry when I disobeyed her by crawling through the fox's burrow to look at Hallows. Granny had known so many things — was it possible that she had somehow forseen the tragedy that was to come? Yet how could she, when I had caused it by my wickedness? I was wicked, wanton, and I had made Justin commit a sin which he would think unforgivable — but he must never know!

"It is too late," I said.

Geraint looked at me, pity in his eyes. "No, Jalinda, it is never too late to make amends. You cannot undo what is done, but God, in his mercy, will forgive you. But you must tell Justin at once."

I stared at him. He was so strong and he was offering me a way of escape. I knew he was right, but I could not accept it. It was too sudden, too terrible. I remembered Selina's face when she learnt of our betrayal and I was tormented by Sir Ralph's agony as he lay dying. If I left Justin now, it had all been for nothing. But if he remained in ignorance we could go on as we were. I was already damned — one more sin would make little difference.

I turned aside so that Geraint should not see my face, for I could not meet his eyes as I said: "No. No one else knows of this and there is no proof. Mayhap you misunderstood Sir Ralph.

It must be so, he would have told me if it were true."

"Jalinda," he said, his voice reproachful. "Do you really believe I would lie to you? Sir Ralph told me everything, though it was not something he was proud of — but he felt it his duty to tell me when I asked for you. He fell in love with your mother when he was young. She wanted him to acknowledge you, but he refused because it would hurt his wife. He offered your mother money, but she threw it in his face, then she ran away. Later — after his wife died — he sought your mother out, but found she had married a good man who had taken you as his own. Then, when he discovered you at the mercy of that mob, he was happy to repay the debt he felt he owed your mother."

"It doesn't matter," I cried, "as long as Justin never learns the truth — and I shall not tell him!"

He looked shocked, but I was defiant now.

"You cannot mean it, Jalinda. When

you knew nothing it was bad enough, but now . . . "

"I don't care. I love Justin. I cannot give him up!"

"It is wrong — can't you see that?" I tossed my head. "If you tell Justin, I shall deny it. I shall swear that you lie because you are jealous of him!"

He looked at me, and the expression in his eyes frightened me. I almost cried out that he was right and I would do as he bid me, but my wilful pride held me silent. And then it was too late.

"I thought I loved you — wanted you above all others as my wife," he said, and the bitterness in his voice seared me like a red-hot flame. "But I did not know you — you sicken me. I will keep your secret. Live as you please and may your soul receive its just deserts! Love you? I despise you, madam! I had thought you had more courage than to hide behind a lie!"

He strode away, leaving me staring after him in anguish. His words rang in my ears, wounding me with the depth of his contempt. I felt a crushing pain in my chest which seemed to threaten my very life.

"You sicken me — I despise you!" he had said.

I despised myself.

I longed to run after him, to beg him to forgive me. But it was much too late. To gain my own way I had destroyed Selina and killed my own father. Was I to throw it all away for the sake of my eternal soul, which was already damned?

I forced myself to stop trembling, waiting until the sickness passed; then I walked slowly back to the house. As I entered the morning-room, Justin glanced up from his book with that lazy smile of his and my heart contracted with pain. He lay down the book and came to me.

"Geraint has arrived," he said with pleasure. He laughed, gesturing towards the book. "I was just trying to find a quotation he used, but I cannot trace it . . ."

"Oh — what was that?" I asked warily.

"I don't really know," he said. "We were speaking of you and he said something — smiling the way he does — and I thought it must be some sort of compliment to you. I must ask him where it comes from . . . "

"Oh, I shouldn't do that, Justin," I said. "He will think you a fool for not understanding the first time."

"Do you think so?" he asked, looking hurt.

I took his arm, forcing myself to smile. "Never mind," I said, using all my art to persuade him. "You must think of one to fox him." I did not want him asking Geraint too many questions.

He smiled, his sunny nature restored. "That is a good idea, Jalinda. You must help me choose."

I laughed and agreed. We began to quote various passages to each other until we found one which we thought might cause Geraint to stop and wonder. But we were wrong. When Justin quoted it later, he placed it at once.

"There! You see, Jalinda, it is impossible to best him," Justin said, turning to Geraint with a wry grin. "I could not place your quotation, cousin. Jalinda said you would think me foolish if I admitted it. Come — tell me from where it originates?"

"Really, Justin — you mean you do not know?" Geraint raised his brow mockingly. "I am sure Jalinda knows."

I flushed, not meeting his eyes. "I am afraid I must give you best in this, Geraint," I said, trembling as I awaited his answer. Would he betray me?

"You surprise me," he replied coldly. "But then — you are full of surprises."

My husband looked at me proudly. I dare not look at Geraint's face for fear of what I might see. My heart was pounding and the palms of my hands were wet with sweat.

"Jalinda would appear to be all that a man could desire," went on Geraint, an odd note in his voice. "You could be called a fortunate man, cousin."

I cursed myself for my weakness but something inside me forced me to look at him then. The scorn in his eyes made me shiver and I turned away quickly, hiding my shame.

Justin did not notice the constraint between us. In his innocence he believed Geraint had paid me a pretty compliment and he was still a little jealous of his wife.

* * *

So Geraint did not betray me and my secret was safe for the time being. Unfortunately for me, my conscience began to make itself felt again. And though I had so defiantly told Geraint that the knowledge of my close relationship to Justin would make no difference, I was soon to find that it did.

When Justin came to me that night, I felt chilled, unable to respond to his caresses. He noticed the change at once — I had always been so eager for his embrace. I apologised, blaming the advanced state of my pregnancy. Justin smiled and kissed me tenderly, accepting my excuse.

After he left me, I cried bitterly, wondering if I would ever feel the old stirring in my blood when he held me. I had a feeling I should not. I loved him, but something inside me had changed. Was it conscience — or was it due to an entirely different reason? I could not forget the excitement I had felt when I first saw Geraint in the garden. Could it be that already I had begun to tire of Justin? No! Oh, please, no! Forgive me, Selina, forgive me! I shook my head in the darkness; I would not admit this — I could not!

The next night, when my husband came to my bed, I felt exactly the same. I shuddered as he touched me and I saw the hurt in his eyes.

"What is the matter?" he asked.

"Nothing. I'm tired, that's all," I

lied, turning my face into the pillow.

"Are you sure?" he said, and his voice was not quite so tender as it had been the night before.

"I am tired, very tired," I repeated and he had to be satisfied with that, though he was hurt and suspicious as he left me. I wondered how long I could keep up this pretence: Justin would not be put off with weak excuses for long. I was suddenly afraid of our life after the child was born.

* * *

Thérèse was married, first in the village church, with friends to lead her by a bride-lace tied with rosemary; then in the chapel with Justin, Geraint and I as witnesses of her true marriage. During the ceremony I saw Geraint watching me and I felt ashamed and ill. As soon as the blessing was over, I complained of feeling weary and went to my room, alone.

I lay on the bed for almost two

hours, thinking deeply and sore at heart. Geraint had been right from the beginning: I could not go on with this marriage to a man who was my half-brother.

My decision taken, I had a feeling of peace. I rose, washed my face in cold water and went downstairs. Justin, Thérèse and her husband were there, and Stefan went immediately to fetch me a chair.

"I hope you are feeling rested, sister," he said kindly.

As if ashamed, Justin hastened to my side, moving the firescreen so that I was protected from the heat of the flames. I smiled at him, my heart aching as I thought of how hurt he would be when I told him the truth.

"Thank you, I am better, Stefan," I said, looking about the room. "Where is Geraint?"

Stefan seemed embarrassed. "I told him you would wish to see him before he left — but he did not want to disturb you, Jalinda. I am sorry, but he left half an hour ago."

"Gone? Geraint gone?" I repeated blankly. "But he was to stay another day . . . "

Stefan avoided my eyes. "He left you his apologies — but there was urgent business awaiting him at home . . . " He broke off awkwardly and I knew that he was lying. Geraint had waited to see his brother wed, then he wasted no time in leaving this house. And I knew why: he despised and hated me.

"Home — you mean he has gone back to France?"

Stefan nodded. I stared at him blindly, seeing only a mist which threatened to envelop me and drag me down into the abyss opening before me. I was too late! How I wished that I had listened to Geraint in the beginning. I had been wilful and heedless — now I should have to pay the price. It would have been hard enough to face Justin with Geraint by my side — but alone! — I did not know if I had the courage to do it.

Justin was looking at me intently. I tried to smile at him, but it was a poor effort and he frowned. Then Stefan reached inside his doublet, bringing out a small silver box.

"I almost forgot," he said. "Geraint asked me to give you this, Jalinda. It is a bride-gift. He meant to give it to you himself . . . " He smiled apologetically as he handed me the casket.

My hands trembled as I took it. I knew Geraint had not forgotten, nor had he intended it as a bride-gift but as a betrothal token. I opened the jewelled clasp and looked inside, catching my breath as I saw the fine gold chain and the pendant of dark green jade in the shape of a heart. In its absolute simplicity it was a thing of great beauty and, as I stared at it, I felt a stab of pain in my heart. I read the enclosed message, hot tears scalding my eyes. I blinked them back.

"Let me see." Justin held out his hand. I gave him the pendant and the note and he read it aloud: "To Jalinda with my sincere wish that she may receive all she deserves in this life and the hereafter. This poor gift is no match for the green of her eyes, nor the stone for the heart that beats in her breast."

Justin watched me closely, and I knew he was jealous. He thought it a pretty compliment and he wanted to see what I felt about Geraint's gift. I tried to smile, but I could hardly keep from crying. So Geraint believed my heart was harder than the green jade, did he? Harder than a stone valued for this very quality. It was a cruel, cruel way of telling me how much he despised me.

"It is very beautiful," said Justin, his voice cold.

"Yes — I suppose it is." I took it from him and laid it down carelessly.

Justin was pleased by my apparent indifference, but Stefan looked hurt. No doubt he thought me callous to treat his brother's gift so disparagingly.

Let him think it! Geraint's cruel words had filled me with a black despair.

Soon after this, Thérèse and Stefan left. I kissed her goodbye, noticing vaguely that she was pale and quiet; but I was too wrapped up in my own misery to be of any help to her. How could I give her hope for the future when my world lay in ruins? She had chosen the path of duty and perhaps she was wiser than I — I was no longer sure of anything.

Justin was glad they had gone. He wanted to be alone with me, to find out why I had been behaving so oddly lately. He put his arms around me, trying to tease me and kiss me into a good humour, but I pulled away from him.

"Leave me alone, Justin — please."

"But I want to kiss you," he said, his face sulky. "I don't think you love me any more — you have changed since Geraint came . . . "

My heart thumped madly. I knew that I ought to tell him the truth now, but I was afraid. Supposing he sent me away — where would I go? I could not face life in Granny's cottage after living at Hallows for so long — but what else could I do? If I had obeyed Geraint he would have protected me, even though he despised me. But he was on his way to France. I found that my courage had deserted me. I could not tell Justin, not yet. Perhaps later, after my child was born.

"I am sorry, Justin. It is just that I have been feeling so ill, but it will soon pass . . . " I smiled at him and his scowl disappeared.

"Why didn't you tell me? I am a selfish brute — forgive me, please," he cried.

I blushed, ashamed of my lies, but the quarrel was over and he was my loving husband again. He was sorry for his flash of temper and anxious to prove how repentant he was. I writhed with guilt as he fussed over me and I was nearly driven mad by his constant attentions. I was glad when fate came to my aid in the guise of the King's messenger.

Justin was summoned to court. He had to leave immediately and he did not know when he would return. The war we had talked of so often had become a reality, and the King was gathering his forces.

Our quarrels were all forgotten as Justin kissed me goodbye. Perhaps because he was going away and I was anxious for his safety I clung to him with some of my old warmth; for I still loved him, only now it was in a different way. I no longer wanted to lie in his arms, but I should never forget that he had saved my life, nor the kindness he had always shown me.

"I thought you had tired of me," he said, holding me tightly, "that you had begun to love another."

"I love no one but you, Justin. I shall never stop caring for you." It was true: I did love him and I dare not examine my feelings for Geraint — it hurt too much.

His eyes lit up with joy. "I thought you wished you had waited and married Geraint. I was sure that was why you turned from me when he was here."

He was going away; now was not the time to burden him with what could only hurt him. I was not sure the time would ever come. I reached up and kissed him lightly.

"I have always loved you, Justin. If I were free to choose and love as I wished, it would always have been you."

He looked so happy that my heart ached for the pain I had caused him, and that I would give him in the future. But I smiled as he rode away and waved to him, then I turned back to Hallows and the loneliness which awaited me there.

For now there would be no loving husband to tease and care for me, no gallants to dance attendance on my slightest whim. I was alone, without even Thérèse's unwilling company. And it was now that Hallows began to seem a big, empty, ugly place, full of shadows and memories which haunted me as I wandered its passages, seeking forgetfulness. But I could not escape myself. As the weeks passed and the birth of my child approached, I became ever more conscious of what my wickedness had brought me to; and I longed for, yet feared, the coming ordeal.

* * *

My child was born and died in the space of a single breath. I wished that I had died, too. They took my son away, refusing to let me see him how ever hard I begged.

"'Tis best you do not see him," said Mrs. Beeson, her face grim. "'Tis for your own good."

I stared at her and then I wept.

Father Renard came to visit me. I saw the sorrow in his gentle eyes and I knew that something had been terribly wrong with my baby.

"God has been merciful," he said. "You must try to accept it, my child."

I turned my face to the pillow, but I did not ask to see my son again. After a while I ceased to grieve, but I had reached a decision: there would be no more children of our union. I would never live as Justin's wife again.

I asked Father Renard to write to my husband and tell him of his son's death.

"Will you not send him word yourself?"

"I cannot — will you do it for me, please?"

"As you wish, my child." He sighed and made the sign of the Cross over me, then he went away.

In time, Justin wrote to me. It was a tender letter, full of his love and concern. It tore at my heart, wounding me deeply. He told me to bear my sorrow bravely and remember we should have other children — would it were possible! — and he blamed himself for being absent when I needed him; ending with a promise to return as soon as he could.

He was in the north with the King; whence our sovereign had marched after it became impossible to treat with Parliament any longer. The situation had worsened following the impeachment and subsequent execution of the Earl of Strafford; and, with fears of an impending impeachment of his Queen in mind, the King attempted to arrest five Members of the Commons. The result was an open breach betwixt King and Parliament, leaving His Majesty no way to go but to the field of battle.

I did not reply to my husband's letter. What I had to tell him must be said face to face and could not be written in a letter.

★ ★ ★

In the October of that year the war began. A battle was fought at Edgehill, resulting in victory for neither side. The King retired to Oxford for the winter, there he planned to muster his forces in preparation for a new campaign the following spring.

Justin came home, bringing the King and a party of gentlemen with him. They had come to inspect some fortress or other — I know not which. It was men's business and interested me little. My heart was too full of my own sorrow to take much interest in the war at that time. However, I did manage to listen to enough of their talk to know that they were still confident of winning in the end. They were a merry company and I was happy to have them at Hallows. At least for a while I could try to forget the grief which was tearing me apart.

His Majesty was a charming and gracious guest. I was honoured by his presence in our home and eager to show my loyalty. But he brushed all talk of the war aside and spoke privately to me, so kindly that his sympathy brought tears to my eyes.

"It is a great sorrow to us that you

should lose your first child, Mistress Frome," he said. "We understand your sadness, but you are young and in good health — you will have others . . . "

He smiled at me and I could only thank him for his concern and agree. I could tell no one the real reason for my grief, except the one who must be told, how ever hard that might be. And I knew it would be hard. I had realised how painful it would be as soon as I saw the welcoming light in my husband's eyes.

He swept me off my feet, kissing me passionately. "My love," he whispered, "it has been so long . . . "

"Justin — His Majesty . . . " I warned, pulling away from him and flushing.

"His Majesty sees and approves," said a voice behind me. "The Queen is gone to France on our behalf — but we miss her sorely."

I turned and, seeing that it was His Majesty's eldest son, I dropped a small curtsy.

The King smiled. "Charles speaks truly, ma'am. We give you our permission to welcome your husband properly."

Justin kissed me again while the King's gentlemen looked on, laughing and jesting good-naturedly. I had no choice but to smile and pretend to be pleased. Oh, how I wished that Geraint had never told me the truth, or that Sir Ralph had been no more than the kind stranger I had thought him. How warmly I would have welcomed my handsome young husband then!

I waited in dread for the time when we should be alone and I must reveal the terrible truth to my husband — a husband who had no right to be mine! How was I to find the courage I so sorely needed?

That night I went to my room with a heavy heart. Justin was not long in following me, and I trembled as I saw the eager light in his eyes. For a moment I was tempted — no one would know the truth if I did not tell him — but, as I looked at him,

I knew that my love had changed. I still loved him, but it was the love of a sister for a dear brother. Why had I not seen it before and saved us all so much misery?

The temptation to go to his arms had gone and I knew it would not return. I must tell him the truth and accept the consequences — whatever they might be. I drew away from him and, in a halting, tear-caught voice, I told him what he had to know. It was hard and it hurt us both deeply. As I watched the glow of love fade from his eyes I felt that I should never know happiness again. I raged at the cruelty of fate who had brought us together, only to fling us apart again. But in my heart I knew that it was I who must bear the blame, and it was I who must live for ever with Justin's heartbreak on my conscience.

He stared at me, horror and disbelief written on his face. How my heart ached for his pain. At first he would not believe me: he had known that

Geraint was to be my betrothed, his father had told him that much and no more, and he accused Geraint of lying. "He wanted you himself," he cried. "This is a wicked lie!"

I looked at him sadly. I, too, had wondered at the start, but in my heart I knew that Geraint was not capable of such baseness, and Justin must know it also. His face was white and there was shame in his eyes, even as he tried to persuade me that it could not be true. He was stunned, shocked, angry. I asked him to go and, after some argument, he left.

I lay on my bed, wishing that I could weep, perhaps tears would ease this ache in my heart, but all mine had long since dried. I could only lie there in the darkness and remember the look on Justin's face. But at last I fell into an uneasy sleep and it was towards dawn when I suddenly awoke to find Justin by my side. He put his arms around me, covering my face with passionate kisses. I thrust him away and leaping out of bed, lit the candle with shaking hands.

"What are you doing?" I cried. "You know this is wrong — we can never be together as man and wife again."

"But I want you, Jalinda. I need you!" he said, his face twisted with pain.

"I know. I still love you, Justin, but my love has changed, as yours will in time. We have sinned but we did not know what we did. You must pray for forgiveness and forget me. I can never have another child of yours — think of what might happen! Besides, you could not live with the knowledge of such sin . . . "

"I can. I will!" he vowed. "If we had a child it might be perfectly healthy . . . "

"I won't take that chance, Justin."

He stared at me for a while; then he came to me and drew me close to him, forcing my head back and pressing his mouth hard on mine. I stood cold and still, unmoving in his arms.

"Jalinda — please," he whispered.

I remained quite still and he fell on his knees before me, burying his face against my flesh and begged me to love him. Oh, how he begged and pleaded, the tears running down his cheeks. My heart broke and broke again to see him humbled and degraded in this way! I would have gone to him then if I could, no matter what the cost to our eternal souls; but he wanted my lips to be warm and eager as they had always been, and I could not give him what I did not have to give.

"Please love me, Jalinda," he wept, "don't deny me — please!"

"I can't, Justin," I whispered. "I'm sorry, so sorry . . . "

He saw then that it was hopeless, and there was bitterness in his eyes. "I think I hate you," he said as he left. But he could not hate me as much as I hated myself.

The next day I hardly knew how to face him, but he greeted me with deadly politeness in front of our guests.

160

I held my head proudly, smiling as if nothing was wrong and hid my pain.

He avoided me as much as possible, but I sought him out. "Justin — we must talk . . ."

"What is there to talk about? I think you said it all last night."

"Please — we can't leave it like this. I want to make amends if I can . . ."

"I have nothing to say to you."

He pushed past me and strode off to rejoin his friends. But that night he came to my room and I knew that he had been drinking heavily. He began to persuade me that Geraint had lied once more.

"He always wanted you," he said, his voice thick and slurred. "He was jealous because you married me, so he invented these foul lies. Do you think my father would not have told me the truth?"

"Perhaps he was ashamed to tell you, Justin," I said. "Geraint would not lie in such a vile way. He could not — he is too fine a person to stoop so low."

It was a mistake to defend Geraint so fiercely. I had forgotten Justin's jealousy, and that he had a temper when aroused. He looked at me and I saw the jealous fury burning in his eyes. "Now I understand!" he cried. "You wish you had married him instead of me. This is a plot between you, to make me believe our marriage is sinful so that you can go to him! I knew you wanted him when he came for Thérèse's wedding. Tell me the truth, you bitch, tell me!" He grabbed my arm, his fingers biting cruelly into my flesh. "I'm waiting!"

"You can't believe that, Justin. I loved you so much . . . " I broke off, wincing with pain as he shook me.

"You are lying," he said, his voice bitter. "You think I am a fool, but you don't deceive me!"

I wrenched away from him. His face was white with anger and, looking into his eyes, I read his intentions there! "No — please don't," I cried, backing away from him in horror.

He laughed harshly. "Afraid, Jalinda? You never were before."

"No, Justin — please!" I pleaded, but to no avail. He seized me and threw me on the bed; then he took me brutally, with no trace of tenderness. For a while I struggled wildly, but he slapped my face, making me cry out with pain; then I just lay still and let him have his way. It was useless to resist; he was so much stronger than I. But he had no joy of me.

Afterwards he stood looking at me coldly, a cruel expression on his face. I did not recognise him; he was no longer the man I had loved, but a bitter stranger. And I had made him what he was.

"You are mine, Jalinda," he said. "My wife, my property, to do with as I will. I shall never let you go, no matter how much you lie or beg. For one thing it would cause a scandal — for another, I would rather see you dead than in my cousin's arms! I leave with the King tomorrow, but when the war is over I shall come back — and I shall take what is mine!"

I stared at him, horrified. He could not mean it! But he did. "You cannot hold me against my will!" I cried.

"You think not? You cannot go to Geraint — for if you do I shall follow and I will kill him. But not you — Oh, no, not you, my dearest wife. You shall come back with me. Wherever you go I will find you, I promise you that."

"But, Justin — you can't live with this on your conscience . . . "

"Be quiet, woman! I have heard enough of your lies!" he shouted.

But I had seen a flash of fear in his eyes and I knew he would be haunted if he carried out his plans, for he was a good Catholic. "I will stay here as your wife in name only," I said. "There will be no scandal — but that is all. You know that is how it must be."

"We shall have time enough to talk when I return," he replied, but his voice had softened, and I knew that he had begun to regret and to suffer for the sin we had committed.

"I give you my word, Justin — I will not go to Geraint."

He looked at me in silence for a while, then he nodded his head and left the room. It was the last time I saw him alone before he went away to the war.

★ ★ ★

The King's party departed the next morning, and I was sorry to see them go. I was especially loathe to part with the dark-haired boy who would one day come to his father's throne. He was a merry child with deep, sparkling eyes and an infectious charm which was to make him the darling of the ladies in the future years.

His Majesty was in need of monies to equip his army. Justin gave him the silver, even that from the chapel. And I — I gave my jewels, just as every other loyal Royalist lady was giving hers. I gave everything, save my wedding-ring and the jade heart. This I kept, though I hardly knew why, unless it was to remind me of what my selfishness had brought to both myself and others.

The King thanked me graciously, bestowing a smile on me. "I wish I had more to give you, Sire," I said, curtsying reverently. "I would I were a man so that I could offer my sword in your cause. I would give my life willingly for you . . . "

"You are as loyal as you are beautiful, Mistress Frome," he replied, giving me his hand to help me rise.

I flushed, kissing his hand and thinking myself well repaid for my humble gift.

The Prince made me a courtly bow and kissed my hand. "We shall never forget your kindness, Mistress Jalinda," he said, and he was every inch as royal as his father.

I smiled and, on a sudden impulse, I bent to kiss his cheek. To my surprise he kissed me back, full on the lips.

The King laughed and his gentlemen thought it a great jest. I laughed too, but Justin scowled. He was even jealous of this child.

So they rode away and Justin went with them. I tried to make my peace with him when he left, but he would not listen and we parted in bitterness. I little knew how many years would pass before we met again.

5

"**G**OOD-DAY, Mistress Frome," said Ben, helping me dismount from my horse.

"Thank you, I will see you tomorrow."

I watched him remount, noticing the lines of pain in his homely face. He was a tall man, thin, with dark, close-cropped hair and proud eyes. Turning his horse, he rode away and I stared after him, wondering how I should have fared without him these past months. It was more than two years now since Justin left to fight for the King, taking most of the men from the estate with him.

Only the women, children and the old remained. But we still had to go on living; the fields must be planted, the harvest gathered and the stock tended. At first I tried to run the estate myself, rising at dawn and seldom returning to the house before dusk. I worked hard those first months, in an effort to forget my grief, but the harvest was poor in spite of all my work. The village people disliked me, and they neglected their tasks, making all manner of weak excuses for their laziness. What I needed was a man with a sound knowledge of the land, but all the men had gone to the war, be it with the King or the rebels.

I was shamed to think that 'Hallows people' had turned against the King; but so it was, not only here but throughout the length and breadth of England. We were a divided nation: father against son, and brother against brother.

So for a time I struggled alone, then I found Ben. He could not join His Majesty's forces, nor yet the Puritans either. He was lame from birth and he dragged his foot along the ground as he walked. He could not march and fight with rest of the men, so he stayed at home and dwelt bitterly on his misfortune. Then I gave him a horse and taught him to ride it. On the ground Ben might be a poor, despised creature whom others mocked; but astride a horse he was as good as any man. I made him my foreman and gave him charge of the estate.

Ben understood the land, as I did not. He also understood the villagers and he knew how to make them work for him. And so we prospered at Hallows, though we heard tales of neighbouring houses being ransacked and cattle stolen in the name of Parliament. But fate smiled on us and we were safe.

On this bleak February afternoon, I watched until horse and rider were out of sight; then, sighing, I went up to the house, unwilling to face the loneliness which awaited me within its walls. I was tired and depressed and I wondered if it was all worthwhile. Perhaps it would be simpler to walk into the sea until the pounding waves dragged me down. True it would be another sin to add to my long list; but then it would all be over and I should sin no more, nor would I hurt anyone ever again. I pushed the thought aside as I always did: somewhere inside me there was a spark of fight left, and I knew that I should never take the easy way out.

Entering the house, I sensed the change of atmosphere at once. There was an urgency, a bustle and a stir which was unusual at this hour of the day. Then Mrs. Beeson came hurrying into the hall and I called to her, asking what was happening.

She smiled. "'Tis Mistress Thérèse and her husband," she said. "They have but this minute arrived and await you in the parlour . . . "

"Thérèse — Stefan?!" I cried gladly and hurried to meet them, not stopping to tidy myself or put off my safeguards.

Thérèse turned to look at me as I burst into the room. She was just as I remembered her: slight and delicately pretty. I held out my arms impulsively and she ran to embrace me. She was laughing and crying at the same time, as was I. We clung to each other with a warmth we had never known in the days before the war. I felt she had become softer, less confident, and it was obvious that she was as pleased to see me as I was to see her.

"Thérèse — Stefan! It is so good to see you. You must forgive my appearance but I could not stay to tidy myself when I knew you were here. Oh, there is so much I want to know — you must tell me everything at once!"

Thérèse laughed. "I have come to ask if you will let me stay here with you."

"Stay with me?" I echoed. "Of course you can — you are more welcome than you know. But I thought you happily settled at Oxford?"

She blushed and it was Stefan who answered for her. "Thérèse is with child, Jalinda. She has been unwell and the life at court is too tense for her just now; besides, I am leaving and she cannot stay there alone. Will you take care of her for me?"

"Willingly, Stefan. You cannot imagine how much it means to me to have her here at Hallows."

"You see, Thérèse," he chided her with a gentle smile. "I told you Jalinda would be pleased to see you." He looked rather conscious as he explained: "She was afraid she might be a burden to you."

I laughed at this. She little knew how desperately I longed for companionship.

"Nonsense! Thérèse must always be welcome here — but she will never be more so than she is today, I promise you."

"Thank you, Jalinda."

She smiled at me and embraced me again. Perhaps because we had not seen each other for a long time, or perhaps because she had been ill, her attitude towards me had completely altered. Once she could hardly bear to speak to me, now she seemed to want to cling to me as if seeking reassurance. I smiled at her, trying to show her that the past was forgotten. Then I turned to Stefan.

"And you, brother — is all well with you?"

He hesitated before answering and there was a flicker of something in his eyes which puzzled me; but he spoke cheerfully enough.

"Yes, Jalinda. I have been lucky so far — the King has had other work for me and I have seen little of the fighting . . . "

I nodded. I knew that both he and Geraint were close to His Majesty, and were often entrusted with important missions. Seeing Thérèse look sharply at him, a flash of fear in her eyes, I wondered why she was afraid — surely Stefan was as safe as any man could be in a country torn by civil war?

I avoided Stefan's eyes as I asked: "Your brother — and Justin, have you news of them?"

"Geraint is well. He was wounded a

few months ago, but is fully recovered now. He sent you his regards and hopes the war has not treated you too harshly." He paused awkwardly, then: "Justin is well, too. He is in the north or he would have come with us . . . "

"Have you seen him recently? Did he send no message for me?" I asked, my throat dry and my heart aching as he was silent.

"He would have come, Jalinda," put in Thérèse, "but he was called away suddenly."

I knew she was lying, but I tried to look as if I believed her. I felt that Justin could have sent a message with them if he had wished — but why should he? I forced myself to smile and changed the subject.

"Does the war go badly for the King? We hear so little here . . . "

Stefan looked grave. "I am afraid the news is not good. Cromwell has turned a rabble into a superior band of fighting men — the Ironsides they call themselves — and so they are. We cannot break them. Our forces are split, trying to defend too many places at one time — the defeat at Marston Moor last July was a disaster. We lost control of the north and we shall not easily recover from its loss."

"Oh — but this is terrible!" I cried.

"And we fare little better elsewhere," he added gloomily.

"I had no idea things were so bad, Stefan. Will we lose the war?"

He shrugged. "Who can tell? It is a possibility we have to face. The Queen has returned to France these many months and His Majesty's heir is safe in Jersey."

I was dismayed. I knew how little that devoted wife would have wanted to leave her husband yet again. If the King had sent her and his sons away, then things had indeed come to a sorry pass!

"Oh, don't! Don't talk of the war any more. I can't bear it — I can't!" Thérèse cried.

I looked at her, surprised. She was

pale and trembling violently. Stefan turned to me, an appeal for help in his eyes. I went to her immediately, taking her in my arms.

"Do not fret, Thérèse. Stefan may be mistaken — anyway, we have much pleasanter things to discuss . . . "

"Have we?" she asked, her face doubtful.

I squeezed her arm gently. "Of course we have — the baby."

"Oh, yes — the baby," she said.

I glanced at her, thinking that she sounded almost reluctant. I made my voice cheerful and light, saying: "And I want to hear all the news from court — I am dying to hear about the latest fashions; it is so long since I saw anyone! It has been so dull here without you, Thérèse. I am so pleased you have come. Now I shall take you up to your room, and we can have a comfortable gossip together."

She smiled faintly and some of the tension went out of her. "I am glad I came, Jalinda."

"Then we are both happy." I laughed and turned to Stefan. "I will see you later. You do not have to leave immediately?"

He shook his head. "No. I have His Majesty's permission to see my wife settled at Hallows."

"How like His Majesty — to think of his friends, even when he is beset by his own problems," I said, and was rewarded with a smile from Stefan.

Thérèse and I went upstairs together, talking of the court and the fashions, which, I learned, had not changed so very much these past three years. The courtiers had other matters to concern them now. However, Thérèse had brought me a gift of some fine orris lace, which Geraint had purchased in France. It was exquisite and I thanked her gratefully: it was a long time since I had thought of any new finery.

We were unpacking her trunks when she suddenly sat down on the bed and burst into tears. I put my arms around her, holding her close until the storm of weeping passed.

"Why are you so unhappy?" I asked, when she was calmer.

"Stefan is going to join Prince Rupert's forces — they are sorely pressed and Stefan volunteered. Why did he have to do that? He was safe with the King, and his work was important — so why must he fight? It is so silly!" Her expression was a mixture of fear and anger.

"Perhaps he needs to fight, Thérèse. If things are as bad as he believes . . . "

"What good will it do if he dies in a lost cause?" she asked. "He should think of me and his child. I miscarried last time, and nearly died of it. He knows that — so how can he leave me?"

She looked so young and defenceless that I felt sorry for her. "I can't answer that, Thérèse, only Stefan knows why he has to go. But there is no need to despair — why should he die? Both Justin and Geraint have fought and they are still alive . . . "

"Stefan isn't like them," she said. "He was never meant to be a soldier. He will be killed — I know he will!"

She was crying again. I took her hand and held it firmly. "Now, listen!" I said. "Your husband may live, but if you carry on like this, your baby will not. You do want your child, don't you?"

She stopped crying and looked at me. "Yes, I want my baby."

I smiled at her. "Good. Then we must see that you take care of yourself." I pulled back the bedcovers. "If I were you, Thérèse, I should get into bed and try to rest. You are worn out. Mrs. Beeson will bring you food and something to make you sleep — and in the morning you will feel much better."

"I am not hungry, Jalinda. But you are right, I am tired. I haven't slept properly for weeks."

"Then it's no wonder you are exhausted. I promise you that you will sleep tonight."

"If you say so," she said meekly, looking at me trustingly.

I squeezed her hand and she gave me a watery smile. Then I left her and went down to the kitchen to find Mrs. Beeson. I asked her to take Thérèse a warm drink and a small dose of the cure I made from poppies.

"She is tired and upset," I said, "it will help her to sleep."

"The poor lass — it's the fault of this wicked war, mistress, that's what it is! I'll go up to her myself . . . "

I heard her muttering to herself as she set about preparing Thérèse's drink. It was evident that she intended to cosset her: well so much the better, Therese would need a great deal of care if she was to bear a living child.

Therese was in good hands, so I went back to the parlour. As I expected, Stefan was pacing about the room and he turned to me anxiously, asking:

"How is she?"

"She is worn out with the journey — and fretting."

He sighed, looking unhappy. "I know . . . "

"How long has she been like this, Stefan?"

"Months — but it has got much worse lately," he replied, his eyes strained. "I wanted to send her to my mother in France but she refused to go. I hope you don't mind us descending on you with no warning, Jalinda. I know times are hard and . . . "

"Oh, we manage well enough. This year's harvest was better than last, and Ben says the granaries are nearly full . . . "

He stared at me in astonishment. "You don't mean you are still working all the fields?"

I was amused by his incredulous look. "We left the bottom meadow fallow this year — but Ben says it will be all the better for it next year."

"Ben — who is Ben?"

"He is my foreman. I make the decisions of course, but . . . "

"You make the decisions?"

"Yes." I smiled slightly. "Did you think I would just stand by while everything went to rack and ruin? If Justin is not to find himself a pauper when he returns something must be done."

He laughed. "You are full of surprises. I believe Geraint once said something of the sort — but I doubt if even he thought you capable of this."

"Geraint knows me better than you, Stefan," I said, my voice dry. "Would you care to take a ride with me and see for yourself?"

He nodded. "Yes, I should like that, Jalinda."

So we rode round the estate together, though it was growing late. He marvelled to see the fields in good heart, the barns stuffed with grain, and the fat cattle grazing by the stream. In fact he was so full of compliments that I began to laugh.

"No, no, Stefan. It is Ben who deserves your praise, not I. I could not have done it without him."

"But you gave him the chance to prove himself, Jalinda. Few people would have done that . . . " His voice was warm, and his eyes reflected that warmth.

We had returned to the house by now, and I could not help noticing the way he looked at me. There was admiration in his face and something else, too. My heart missed a beat; it was a long time since a man had looked at me that way.

"Jalinda . . . " he breathed, taking two steps towards me. "Justin is a fool to stay away all this time. If you were my wife I would find a way of coming to you."

His words brought me quickly to my senses: I knew why Justin did not come. I walked to the buffet and poured some wine into a glass. My back was turned to him as I said:

"I trust Justin will be pleased with me. I think I have been a dutiful wife — and I hope I always shall be . . . "

When I handed him his wine he was looking rather ashamed of himself. I smiled at him. I did not blame him, indeed I understood: Thérèse would not be particularly responsive just now, and I could easily have given him what he asked, for I, too, had a need. But at last I had learnt that what I wanted was not necessarily the most important thing. I would not seduce Thérèse's husband while she lay in a drugged sleep upstairs.

We ate our meal together, talking of the war and of Stefan's desire to prove himself.

"I cannot stay at Oxford now," he said. "If I was not needed — if the war was going well — it might be different. But if I do not go I will always feel that I neglected my duty, that I was a coward. Do you understand, Jalinda? I know my wife does not . . ."

"She loves you, Stefan, it is natural that she should be anxious for you."

"If I could be sure of that, perhaps I would not have to go . . ."

I stared at him in surprise. "Of course she loves you — she is almost mad with fear for you!"

"Fear for me — or for herself if I should die?" he asked, sounding bitter. "Oh, she doesn't want me to leave, but she doesn't want me near her either. She was never a very loving wife, Jalinda — and now she can hardly bear me to touch her."

"You should not be telling me this," I said.

"I know — but I wanted you to understand . . . "

"I did understand, Stefan — and I am sorry."

Looking at him then, I realised that he, too, had born his share of disappointment and sorrow. It explained why he had looked at me that way, and why Thérèse had clung to me instead of her husband. Poor Stefan: poor Thérèse. It was ironic really. I was made for love and my husband was denied me; Thérèse had a warm, loving man and she feared his embrace. What a mess we had all made of our lives!

Suddenly I laughed. Tonight I had sacrificed my own desires for someone else, and the funny thing was that Thérèse would not have really cared. Stefan asked me why I was laughing, but I refused to tell him. I still owed loyalty to the girl sleeping so trustingly above in her room, and I knew myself too well.

Stefan studied me in silence. "Jalinda," he said hesitantly. "Is something wrong between you and Justin. I know I should not ask, but you are both dear to me . . . "

"No — of course not," I lied, smiling too brightly. "Justin sends me word whenever he can. He is too busy to come, that's all."

He did not believe me, but he was too kind and too good a friend to call me a liar to my face. I tried to change the subject, asking:

"And Geraint — is he married now?"

Stefan shook his head. "Geraint will

not marry, Jalinda."

My heart contracted with pain and without thinking, I cried: "But he must! He cannot waste his life because . . . " I halted, blushing.

"Because he loves you — is that what you were going to say?"

"Because he once thought he loved me."

"I said loves, Jalinda."

I stood up and began to pace about the room in agitation. Why should Stefan's words cause my heart to beat so wildly, and the pain I had banished begin again?

"You are wrong, Stefan," I said at last. "Geraint hates me. I wear this to remind me of that — and other things . . . " I fingered the jade heart, remembering Geraint's parting message.

"Life can be very cruel," he said, looking at me sadly.

I stopped my pacing and stood gazing up into his eyes. He was tall and the years had given him maturity. I no longer found him dull and I turned away quickly as the flame of desire leapt up in his eyes again. It was time for me to leave. I wished him goodnight and walked towards the door.

"Goodnight, Jalinda," he whispered, and his voice entreated me to stay.

I paused briefly, but I did not look back; for if I had I might have gone to him. He was going to war, perhaps to his death. He wanted something to take with him, a memory which would ease his heart when he was lonely and afraid. How long was it since I had lain in a man's arms? Too long! I was tempted, I confess it. But this was the path to heartbreak and shame, and I was determined to tread it no more. I had stolen Justin from Selina, but I had loved him. I would not take Stefan from Thérèse, just because I happened to be lonely.

"Goodnight, Stefan," I said, and closed the door behind me.

In the morning Thérèse was rested and she was with us all the time. The danger was past, and in my heart I was glad that I had done what was right and not what I had wanted to do.

The next day Stefan left us, and, as he rode away, I had a terrible premonition that we should never see him again.

★ ★ ★

When Thérèse first came back to Hallows she was three months with child; and though I was careful not to show it I was deeply concerned for her. She had suffered a miscarriage once before and I was afraid that it might happen again. She was very nervous and terrified that she would die in childbed.

"I shall not let you die, Thérèse," I told her one morning as we sat together at our sewing. "You are going to live and your son, too."

She laughed. "How can you tell it will be a boy?"

"Because I say so, of course."

"Oh, Jalinda, how confident you are. I wish I was more like you. Geraint told Stefan to bring me here. He said you were strong and would take care of me."

I was surprised. "Geraint said that — are you sure?"

She smiled and nodded her head eagerly. "Oh, yes, I remember it quite well. I was reluctant to come — I was not always kind to you, Jalinda . . ."

"If we were not as close as we should have been, Thérèse, it was as much my fault as yours. I did not make it easy for you, did I?"

"I was jealous of you. I could not understand why my father had taken you in, nor why he made us be your companions. It was stupid and I wish I'd tried harder to be your friend. Will you forgive me, Jalinda?"

I leaned forward and touched her hand. "Please, my dear sister, do not think of it any more. We are friends now and you have no idea how much that means to me."

She smiled and picked up her needlework again. I was silent for a time, thinking of what Geraint had said to Stefan. I could not believe that he had paid me such a compliment: I had earned no praise from him. I fingered the jade heart and sighed. What a fool I was to care what he thought of me!

That morning was typical of our days. We slipped into a quiet companionship, and, as the weeks passed, Thérèse lost her fretful look. Her cheeks bloomed and her eyes regained their former lustre. I spent as much of my time with her as I could, and it was almost as if we were young girls again — except that Selina was not with us . . .

★ ★ ★

Five months went by in this peaceful manner and we almost forgot that our country was at war. But we were soon to have a rude awakening. I was tending my herb garden one morning when I heard the sound of pounding hooves and Ben came riding furiously up to the house. He reined in as he saw me, causing his horse to rear up and froth at the mouth, its sides heaving as if he had pushed it hard.

"You must leave here at once!" he cried. "The Roundheads are coming."

I looked at him in dismay. We had been safe for so long that I had convinced myself that the war would pass us by. But now all my hard work would be destroyed. They would empty the barns, drive off the cattle and ransack the house. I should have failed and Justin would come home to ruin.

I could not let it happen — it should not happen!

"You must take your women and hide," Ben was saying.

I stared at him in a daze, but I knew he was right. The women were more important than the grain and stock — but where could I take Thérèse? She was too near her time to run and hide under a bush; the shock would

likely kill her and the child. I reached
my decision quickly. There was just a
chance that it might all be saved. I
would take that chance. It should be
all or nothing — but I would not think
of failure.

I turned to Ben. "Thank you for
the warning — Now look to your
family."

"But you, mistress . . . ?"

"Can take care of myself. I don't
need you — go on, Ben!"

He hesitated and I knew he was
torn between his loyalty to me and
his family. He had a mother and three
sisters who depended on him. I urged
him to go, and at last he wheeled his
horse about and raced away.

I ran back to the house, going first
to find Mrs. Beeson and warn her of
what I meant to do. She stared at me,
horrified, exclaiming: "You cannot do
it, mistress!"

"What else can I do? Thérèse cannot
ride a horse or hide in a ditch. I must
do it and hope for the best!"

Her penetrating eyes explored my face, seeking for the truth, then she nodded. "You were always a deep one, and I doubt you've told me all — but mebbe you can do it . . . "

I smiled mockingly at her. "Are you afraid I shall betray you all? You wrong me. I will save you if I can — if not . . . "

"Then I shall know what to do — but what of her?"

"You had best not ask."

I saw the horror in her eyes and my head shot up proudly. What right had she to criticise my decisions? — that was something I reserved for myself alone. I left her staring after me and sped up to Thérèse's room. She was resting on her bed with her eyes closed and I remembered that she had earlier complained of a headache. God save she had nothing worse before this day was done!

"Thérèse my dear," I said, as calmly as I could. "I have unpleasant news . . . "

She sat up in alarm. "Not Stefan?!"

I forced myself to laugh. "Oh, no — nothing as terrible as that. We are to have visitors, that's all — some of Cromwell's men."

"The Roundheads are coming here? They will kill us all!"

"Nonsense!" I chided her as if I had no fears of my own. "They only want food and horses. I shall give them what they want and then they will go away."

"But, Jalinda . . . "

"You must stay here, Thérèse. Father Renard will stay with you and you must lock yourselves in until I come to you."

"But what about you?"

"I shall be entertaining our guests." I laughed. "Do not worry, Thérèse, I shall be quite safe. After all, they are Godfearing men, are they not?"

She looked doubtful, but she was used to doing as I told her. I smiled reassuringly at her, then I went to Father Renard. When I told him exactly what I planned, his face paled and he crossed himself.

"I cannot do it!" he cried.

"You are the only man here, Father. It is your duty."

"It would be a stain on my soul."

"I know that," I said quietly. "And if there was any other way I would not ask it of you. But if they refuse to listen to me — then you know what will happen to Thérèse. Will you stand by and do nothing — would that not be just as deadly a sin in God's eyes?"

He regarded me silently for several moments, then he reached out and took the pistol from me. I showed him how to load it, glad now that I had watched Justin so many times in the past.

"You won't fail me, Father Renard?"

"It shall be as you say," he said, shuddering.

"Thank you. Now I must prepare to meet our guests."

I hurried up to my own room and donned my best gown, then I brushed my long hair until it shone, putting on the cap of gold Justin and bought me. I was dressed as fine as if I was to meet the King himself, and no one could doubt that I was a Royalist.

Ready at last, I went downstairs, trying to calm my fluttering nerves. The house was quiet and still, just as it should be. And looking out of the window, I was in time to see a cloud of dust as a troop of horsemen came galloping up to the house.

Then they were in the courtyard, about a score of them. They shouted eagerly to one another as they made for the door, drawn swords in their hands. The sun glinted on their breastplates and strange helmets. It was the first time I had seen the enemy and they were a fiercesome sight. But they were only men, and I had never been afraid of men. I went to the door and flung it open.

"Good-day, gentlemen. I bid you welcome to Hallows," I said, smiling.

They halted abruptly, surprised. I

was plainly a Royalist; my gown and my looks told them that if they had been in any doubt. I had deliberately planned it so, the more to shock them and give them pause. They stared at me as I continued with my speech of welcome:

"My granaries are full, my stock well fatted, and my wine cellar still has a fair sample to offer. I give it to you freely."

One of them laughed harshly. "Give it — we'll take what we want," he said.

There were murmurs of agreement and they moved towards me menacingly. I held my ground, though my heart was racing madly, and pointed the pistol I had kept hidden in my skirts at them.

"One or more of you will die if you wish for the honour of making war on women and children," I said, my voice scornful. "But there need be no bloodshed if you will grant me only one request."

They hesitated, for though they could

easily overpower me, one must die and they did not know how many more pistols were trained on them from the windows of the house. They looked up uneasily, muttering in low voices as if undecided what to do. Then a tall man, with a pale, stern face stepped forward, and I directed the pistol at his heart.

"What would you ask of us, mistress?" he asked.

The other men were silent now and I realised that he must be their leader. I looked into his eyes for a few moments and what I read there made me smile.

"I think you are a man of honour, sir," I said. "We will not resist you — but you must leave my womenfolk alone."

For a second our eyes locked in silent conflict, testing each other's strength. Then he nodded his head. "We are men of God. Cromwell's men. We do not make war on helpless women. If there is no resistance, we will do you no harm."

"Your men will not even touch them!"

"You have my word." He turned to the others. "You heard me — I'll hang the first man who lays a finger on a woman!"

There was a murmur of dissent, but it was obvious from their faces that they knew him to be a man of his word. I breathed a sigh of relief: Thérèse need not die. I stepped back, lowering the pistol. The Roundhead's leader replaced his sword in the leather baldric slung across his chest.

I curtsied to him. "You are welcome to my house, sir. I am Mistress Jalinda Frome. Will you do me the honour of giving me your name?"

"I am Robert Francis. I serve Cromwell and the army. Now, Mistress Frome, you will show me your stores, and mind you hide nothing from me, for I warn you it will go hard with you if you try to cheat me."

"I will hold nothing back, Robert Francis," I said, lifting my head proudly. "I have given my word."

"I have yet to find a Royalist who kept his word!" he said, his face cold.

"Then let us see if a Royalist lady can match a Roundhead captain for honour. If you will come with me I will show you everything."

He bowed stiffly. I asked if I might ride one of his horses and he looked suspicious. "I have no intention of trying to escape — but if you wish to see everything, then I must ride with you," I said.

"I should kill you if you tried to escape me."

I laughed, looking up at him mockingly. "Then it is fortunate that I have more sense than to try, isn't it? Would you be kind enough to assist me, sir?"

He stared at me as if suspecting some trickery, but he helped me to mount. Then he warned three of his men to stay on guard outside the house. The rest of them followed us as we rode out of the courtyard. I think they half expected me to lead them into an ambush — perhaps they imagined I had a troop of cavalry hidden in my barns, I do not know. What I do know is that they could hardly believe their own eyes as they saw the sacks of oats and barley stacked to the rafters. They were astonished at my cattle, pigs and geese. Nowhere else had they found so much: the Royalist ladies either had little left or they hid what they had. I held nothing back.

Exclaiming in glee, they started to load the wagons, and when they had cleared the barns, they rounded up the stock. I was overjoyed as they began to move off. It had worked: they were going! Ten of them rode off with the carts, but the rest remained and my heart sank as Robert Francis spoke. They had decided to use Hallows as a base for their raiding sorties in the neighbourhood.

Robert Francis smiled thinly. "You have kept your word, Mistress Frome. But I must impose on your good nature a while longer. You will prepare a room in your house for me, and my men will use the barns."

"As you wish, sir," I replied, smiling at him. "You will be treated as a guest."

I doubt he truly believed me, but my smile was pleasant and, poor fool, he could not see beneath it to the smouldering anger in my heart. Only one man had ever been able to read what was in my mind if I wished to keep it hidden, and that man was not Robert Francis.

I rode back to the house and released Mrs. Beeson from the kitchen. I told her to prepare the best bedchamber for our guest.

"And tonight you must cook a meal as if it were for the King himself," I said.

"Aye, mistress," she replied. "I'll do as you bid me, though I do not know what you are about. But what would have happened if thy plan had not worked, answer me that?"

"Mr. Renard would have shot Thérèse

and himself. You and the others would have escaped through the passage as we planned — while the Roundheads were busy with me. I think I could have entertained them long enough for you to reach safety."

"Mistress Jalinda! You never meant to . . . ?"

I laughed mockingly. "Since it did not happen you will never know — will you, Mrs. Beeson?"

She clicked her tongue, shaking her head at me but I laughed again. Let her think what she would of me, I did not care! I left her and went up to Thérèse. Father Renard was nowhere to be seen; he had watched me leave with the Roundheads and guessed that all was well, now he was safely hidden in the secret place known only to himself and the family. I would take him food and hope that no one discovered him: it was a chance we had to take.

That evening I dined with Robert Francis alone. Thérèse was feeling ill, and I thought it best she kept to her room as much as possible. The less she saw of the enemy the better. Mrs. Beeson had excelled herself and we dined well.

Robert Francis ate and drank liberally, and, as he drank my best wine, I could see a change in him. His mood grew steadily warmer towards me and I was sure I had not been mistaken in him. But I kept up my modest manner, conducting myself as I knew he would think seemly, speaking little and only for his comfort. As the night wore on he thawed increasingly, talking of the war and boasting of Cromwell's victories. I listened patiently, making no comment; and soon I knew what kind of man he was — and what he thought of me.

In Robert Francis complete opposites were combined in a strange way. By conviction he was a Parliamentarian, by religion a Puritan — but by nature he was a man of lust and passion. His eyes told me that he wanted me. He wanted me so badly that his hands shook and there was a fine sweat on his brow. He could not take his eyes from me; I could feel them burning my flesh, so strong was his desire. I smiled inwardly. I had made one bargain with this man; I would not shrink from others if need be. But I should not be easily won.

"It is late, sir," I said, standing up and curtsying to him. "I must beg you to excuse me now."

He laid his hand on my arm, detaining me. "Must you go?" he asked hoarsely.

I lowered my eyes, pretending to be a little afraid of him. "I am a modest woman, sir. It is not fitting that I should be alone with you so late in the evening — I beg you, let me go."

His eyes devoured my face and his fingers tightened on my sleeve. "The war has been long, mistress. What if your husband no longer lives? I would that you stay with me." His voice had grown urgent, pleading. I wanted to laugh, but instead I said:

"I cannot, sir — do not press me, I

implore you. You gave your word, and I charge you to keep it."

He started and his hand fell back, his face pale in the fire's glow. I saw that I had judged him aright; he would not force me, no matter how great his need. I would take full advantage of that need; I would play upon it and feed it until he was so mad for me that he would do anything I asked! I would give him myself, and he would leave me Hallows, untouched, and with all my barns still standing. It was a good plan, or so I thought, and it might have worked. But in the end I was forced to make a very different bargain with him.

I do not know if I was careless, or whether they had come to know the secrets of our hiding-places. Whatever, they found it and dragged poor Father Renard from his sanctuary. They took him to their leader and he sent for me. When I arrived I saw that they had forced the priest to his knees and were all around him, taunting him cruelly.

"It's a dirty, stinking priest," jeered one of them.

"Aye — watch him tremble and shake."

They all laughed, except Robert Francis; he looked at me and his face was angry. "Do you deny it?" he demanded.

I shook my head: there was no point in lying. "I would speak with you alone, sir," I said.

He hesitated briefly, then he took my arm, pushing me roughly into the next room. "Well?" he asked.

I was silent for a moment, but a cry of fear from the other room made up my mind. "I know you have no love for priests," I began, "but Father Renard is a good man — he never harmed anyone."

He snorted, looking disgusted. "Have you not heard of the Spanish Inquisition — or our own Bloody Mary? Don't you know what those popish devils are capable of? We want no more incense-burning papists in England!"

"Yes. I have heard of these things and I condemn them as much as you — but what has Father Renard to do with such wickedness?"

"He is a Catholic and all Catholics are whining hypocrites. You must know how we feel or you would not have hidden him away. I will overlook it — but he must die. I will keep my word, though you broke yours."

"I kept my word," I cried, lifting my head proudly. "I promised stores, not the life of a priest — And I will make another bargain with you, Robert Francis . . . "

He glared at me. "What can you offer this time? Nothing I have not already taken — unless you cheated me . . . ?"

"I have not cheated you. What I have to give you cannot — will not take."

He did not understand me, so I smiled at him, but it was not the modest smile I had always shown him before. "I will give you your heart's desire, Robert — if you will give me your word the priest shall live." Still he stared at me in silence and I held my breath — had I misjudged him, would his convictions overrule his desires?

"What mean you, madam?" he asked at length.

"I will give you myself." I moved slowly towards him until our bodies almost touched, then I reached up and kissed his cold lips. Suddenly they grew warm and his arms went round me, pulling me hard against him. I looked up into his face and I knew that I had won.

"Very well," he said, releasing me. "But he leaves this house. My men will not harm him but I cannot guarantee his safety through our lines — do you agree to these terms?"

"Yes. One favour I would ask of you — I would see him alone before he leaves."

"Five minutes — no more."

"Thank you."

He went into the other room and I

heard angry voices. His men did not like whatever he was saying to them. I waited in dread, but I need not have worried: he was a law unto himself. In a few moments Father Renard was thrust roughly into the room and the door slammed behind him.

A trickle of blood ran down his cheek and there was a cut on his mouth. I took out my kerchief and wiped the blood away.

"I am afraid they have hurt you," I said. "I know not how they found you — or if I was at fault . . . "

"Nay, 'twas none of your doing. They have learnt to find our hiding-places and I doubt I am the first they've found." He crossed himself and I saw the fear in his eyes. Then I knew that what I had done was well worth the doing. I smiled at him.

"Captain Francis has agreed to let you go. He does not guarantee your safety once you leave here, but you know the countryside so well, and you have a good chance of winning free."

He looked at me sadly, a hint of reproach in his eyes — or was that my imagination? I reached up and undid the clasp of the jade heart. I looked at it with regret: I had never thought to part with it, but it was all I had to give him. I put it into his hand, closing his fingers over it.

"This will pay for your passage to France," I said.

He shook his head and tried to give it back to me. "I cannot take it, Mistress Jalinda. I know you treasure it — you wear it always. You have given so much for me already . . . "

Then I had seen a hint of reproach in his eyes. I laughed merrily. "Given so much, Father Renard? I do not understand you — what do you imagine I have given?"

His face was sad and shame was in his voice as he said: "I am not a fool. I know he would not have given me my life unless he received something in return. And though I am a priest I am also a man and I know other men

213

for what they are. You paid a price for my life and I can guess what that price was. If I were braver I should forbid you to do what you intend — but that is my sin, not yours, and God will punish me."

I could not let him go with this guilt in his heart; he was too honest a man. I laughed again, as if highly amused. "Oh, Father Renard, you shock me, indeed you do! What have I ever done to make you think so ill of me?"

He stared at me, hope dawning in his eyes. "I could never think ill of you," he said. "I know you thought only of me — and I honour you for it."

"For an intelligent man you speak very foolishly, sir. I have given the captain some gold which I had hidden — but of course he does not want to share it with his men, so he did not mention it. Now tell me — where is the sin in that?"

"Is that the truth, Mistress Jalinda?"

I looked boldly into his eyes. "I swear I have given nothing that will harm me or cause me grief. There — will that content you?"

It was the simple truth. I had promised nothing that would cause me grief. He saw that I meant it and, as he did not know me for the wicked sinner I was, he would be at peace. "Then — I thank you. God be with you, my child."

"And with you, Father."

"I shall pray for you as long as I live, Jalinda."

It was the first time he had ever called me simply Jalinda. I kissed his hand and fought back my tears. He was a good man and we should miss him. "Then surely I shall be saved," I said lightly, hiding my feelings. "For God will listen to the prayers of such a truly good man. Now take the pendant and go . . . "

He touched my head gently. "Bless you, my child," he said and then he left.

I watched him pass through the soldiers and I heard the low growl rumbling in their throats. I clenched my hands, wondering if they would change their minds and tear him to pieces. There was hatred on every face, blood-lust in their eyes and I feared for him as they slowly parted to let him through. But I had done all I could — it was in the hands of his god now. And in the end they let him pass.

★ ★ ★

I went to Robert Francis that night, wearing only a night-chemise of tiffany, which clearly showed the curves of my body beneath its filmy folds. He stared at me, almost as though he saw the devil in my slender form; but his desire for me was stronger than his conscience. I had brought wine and he looked at it suspiciously. I had played my part too well and I believe he thought I might seek to take his life and my own, rather than betray my virtue. I smiled, shaking out my long hair as I poured the wine into two goblets and drank from one of them.

"You need not fear to drink, Robert Francis," I said. "I made a bargain with you — and I will keep it."

He laughed then, taking the goblet from me and drinking deeply. The wine warmed him and I saw that his doubts were disappearing. I lay down on the bed, smiling up at him invitingly. Suddenly he threw himself on me with throbbing urgency; thrusting and groaning until he was spent. When he had finished with me I lay still, feeling bruised and violated. Yet somehow his animal lust had answered an aching need in me; and when he came to me a second and third time — taking his pleasure more slowly now — I knew that if he had but had more tenderness in his soul I could have been well satisfied with him as my lover.

He was a man in whom the pleasures of the flesh were strong. But though he longed for the joy I gave him he also feared it; and it was a meeting of our bodies only. I knew there was no lasting

217

joy to be had from such a man, and I was careful to hide my true nature from him. I showed sufficient response to flatter him, but not enough to let him guess that I received as much from our bargain as did he, for only by letting him retain the guilt I knew he felt could I hope to gain yet more advantage from him.

I still had Hallows to think of, and Thérèse, and all my people. And I was determined that when the Roundheads left, my barns would stand untouched and next year's crops continue to grow in the fields. Therefore I must find a way of wringing a third bargain from this man — but what could I find to give him now?

For two weeks more he stayed at Hallows, while his men wreaked havoc on our neighbours. I heard that some of the women were foolish enough to try to defend their homes with force. They paid the penalty, and I shuddered to think what might have happened to us if I had done the same. But they were virtuous women who would never dream of stooping to make a pact with their enemies. I was not. We survived: they did not.

At the end of the two weeks Robert Francis prepared to leave.

"Must you go?" I asked, and my concern was not entirely false.

He smiled, a strange, cunning look in his eyes. Then he turned aside so I could not read his expression as he said: "I regret, Mistress Jalinda, that I must burn the barns and crops before I go."

I gasped. "But we shall starve next winter if you do that!" I cried. "What harm can we do your cause? We are but women and weak, helpless creatures. For pity's sake will you not leave us the crops?" I looked at him pleadingly. "Robert — does what we have had together these past two weeks mean nothing to you?"

"I would leave your fields unburned if I could," he said. "But it is my duty . . . "

I caught at his arm, tears gathering on my lashes. "Is there nothing that will sway you? I would do anything, Robert, anything . . . "

He turned to face me then, a feverish light burning in his eyes. "To show favour to a Royalist could hang me — but I will risk it on one condition . . . "

"Anything, Robert, only leave me Hallows and food for the winter."

"If I come back after the war — and it must end soon — will you come to me?" he asked. "Whether your husband is dead or alive . . . "

I stared at him and for a moment I hesitated. To give a few nights of my life to this cold man was one thing, but to promise him the rest of my days was quite another. Somewhere inside me a voice cried out that it wasn't worth it — let him do as he would with Hallows. But then I thought of Thérèse and her unborn child. If there was no harvest she would starve and all my people, too.

"Come back to claim me, Robert Francis — and I am yours. Only leave me enough stores for the winter."

"Do you swear it by the Holy Book?"

"I do," I answered, casting down my eyes lest he see how little that cost me.

"Then 'tis a bargain, Jalinda. I will leave you the house, crops and barns — more, I will leave you your horse, too."

I saw a flicker of triumph in his eyes and something told me that he had tricked me. He had never meant to destroy Hallows. One day I was to learn that he had reasons of his own for leaving it untouched — except for the chapel, his men smashed that before they went. I suppose he had to let them destroy something or they would have rebelled, and he would take no more risks than he need. I was sorry to see such wanton destruction, but at least the house and the crops were safe.

On the day he finally left I stood and watched them ride away. Then I smiled. If he thought he had bested me he did not know me very well. I had long ago decided never to live as Justin's wife again, and, since in this world I needed a man's protection, as well Robert Francis as any other. Or so I thought then, but I did not yet know his full measure. For the moment I was content to see him go and know that Hallows was still intact. We should not starve and I was prepared to let the future lie in the hands of fate. The war was not over. He might never return — and if he did, well, I would manage somehow.

The enemy were gone. I was alive, young, and life was good. I felt the wind in my hair, my blood tingling in my veins. I began to laugh for pure joy as I ran back to the house.

6

AFTER the Roundheads left, our life gradually returned to normal. They had taken all our stores and most of the valuables from the house, but I did not care that we were near to ruin. For the first time in years I felt something more than the ever-present urge to survive and I started to take an interest in my books and needlework again. I suppose Robert Francis had brought me alive again, making me realise that perhaps my life wasn't over after all.

I had kept my arrangement with him a secret from Thérèse, for I knew she would never understand why I had done it. But I was sure Mrs. Beeson was aware of it from the start. However, she said nothing to anyone and perhaps I imagined that disapproving look in her eyes. Anyway, I did not let it trouble me. My conscience was my own affair.

A week after our uninvited guests departed Thérèse was seized with violent pains. Her child was coming some two or three weeks early. A result of her emotional state these past weeks.

She stood at the top of the stairs, clinging to the balustrade and screaming for me. When I arrived, with half the household in tow, she flung herself on me, weeping hysterically. I tried to calm her as I helped her to bed, but as I turned to leave, she caught at my arm.

"Don't go, Jalinda," she begged. "I'm so frightened. Please don't leave me alone . . . "

"I shall be five minutes, no more — then I shall stay with you until after the child is born. There is nothing to worry about, my dear, I promise you."

Her eyes were wide with fright. "It hurts," she said, plucking at the bedclothes with restless hands.

"I know — but only for a little while, dearest. It will soon be over and then you will have your son to hold in your arms. He is worth a little pain, isn't he?"

"If you say so, Jalinda." She sighed as she lay back against the pillows. She seemed such a child to me, with her soft hair clinging damply to her forehead and the tear-stains on her cheeks. "Hurry back," she said.

"I will." I smiled at her and went to find Mrs. Beeson.

She was in the kitchen, setting water to heat over the fire and as I entered she rushed at me, anxious for news. I told her what she already knew: that Thérèse was in pain and terrified. She shook her head, muttering darkly that she had always known it would come to this. I rebuked her sharply, warning her to hold her tongue. I wanted no gloomy prophecies. Other women might die in childbirth: Thérèse should not. I was not going to let her die!

It was a long and difficult labour. Poor girl; she suffered greatly. It took all my determination and Mrs. Beeson's skill as a midwife to bring her through the ordeal. But, together, we did it, and afterwards we looked at each other in triumph. We might have our differences, Mrs. Beeson and I, but in this we were of one mind.

So Thérèse and her child would both live, just as I had promised her. But I had never doubted it: she was important to me and I refused to let her die.

Her son was small, fair and exactly like his mother. He was a sickly creature at the start and his mother's milk was not enough to satisfy him, so we summoned a wet-nurse from the village. She was a stout, healthy woman who had reared five sons successfully; and young Stefan improved daily.

After a few weeks Thérèse began to recover too. She was pale and listless for a while, but I prepared one of Granny's mixtures and made her drink it every day. She complained about the horrible taste, saying that it made her feel sick. However, it gave her an appetite. She began to eat her food and gradually the colour returned to her cheeks. At first she was content to sit watching her son gurgling in his cot, but then she began to take an interest in her embroidery, and I knew that she was better.

It was late September now and Thérèse had received no letters from Stefan. I tried to tell her that she need not worry, but I could not convince her — perhaps because I could not convince myself. I had a terrible feeling that something was wrong.

★ ★ ★

Three months after Stefan was born we had another visitor. This time Thérèse saw him first and she ran joyfully to meet him. I heard her glad cry and I thought it must be Stefan, so I waited for a few minutes before following her. But as they came into the hall, I could see it was not Stefan but Geraint. I stood absolutely still, my heart thumping painfully.

"It is good to have you at Hallows again, Geraint," I said, not daring to look at him. "Come in and rest — you must be weary with travelling."

"Thank you, Jalinda. It is good to be here with you and Thérèse."

I raised my eyes then and saw that he was smiling. My heart surged with joy and I turned my face away, lest he read the thoughts I would keep hidden in my heart. But already the moment had passed. Thérèse was clinging to his arm and hurrying him up to the nursery.

"You must come and see your nephew, Geraint," she cried eagerly.

He smiled, letting her lead him up the stairs, but I thought I saw a shadow pass across his face. I had a sudden premonition and I knew he brought bad news. I followed them slowly and was in time to see his tall figure bent over the child's cot. He asked to be allowed to hold his nephew and Thérèse proudly placed her son in his arms. At that moment Geraint glanced at me and I gasped as I read the message in his eyes.

He was telling me that it could have been our child he held. And seeing the way he tenderly cradled little Stefan I knew just what I had lost. I turned away as tears suddenly stung my eyes, looking out of the window at the falling leaves and the light mist swirling over the field

Vaguely, I heard Thérèse telling Geraint that it was time for her to take Stefan to his nurse and that she would see him later. A warning sounded in my brain and I walked back to Geraint, so I was by his side when she suddenly stopped in the doorway and looked back.

"I was so excited, I forgot," she said. "Have you seen Stefan — is he well?"

I saw the look on Geraint's face and

I knew at once. I touched his arm, my eyes flashing a warning.

He frowned, hesitating, then: "No, Thérèse, I have not — seen Stefan."

She looked disappointed but not too upset; after all, it was unlikely the brothers would meet. They were fighting in different parts of the country. She went out of the room and the sound of her footsteps receded.

Geraint looked at me. "Why did you stop me?" he asked. "She will have to know."

"Yes — but not like that. I will tell her — believe me, Geraint, I do know what is best for her."

He frowned, studying my face and I felt that he did not quite trust me. "I had thought to tell her myself," he said.

"As you wish." I sighed. "How long can you stay?"

"A few days — but I don't see . . . "

"We will tell her together in a day or so — but let her have the pleasure of your company for a while. Will you do that — please?"

He looked doubtful, but in the end he agreed. Perhaps he found my concern for Thérèse hard to believe; after all, I had never had much time for her in the past.

"What news of the war?" I asked, then laughed. "Forgive me, I am thoughtless. You must be tired and hungry — it is just that we hear so little here . . . "

He smiled. "I am tired, hungry too. But we will talk as I eat. You must be anxious for news."

I sighed. "The war seems to drag on for ever — and what little we do hear is always bad . . . "

He nodded his head, agreeing and I saw he looked weary. I longed to kiss away the lines of strain about his eyes, to touch his hair and hold him in my arms. I restrained myself: I had given up all right to be anything to Geraint — except his cousin's wife. And for that he despised me.

"There is no good news to tell," he

said, following me up to the room which was always kept for him.

There I left him alone, to refresh himself; and after a while he came down, looking with appreciation at the meal Mrs. Beeson had prepared for him.

"'Tis a long time since I have tasted anything as good as this," he said, grinning.

"Then sit and eat."

He took me at my word, and I waited while he ate his fill. He sighed with satisfaction, wiping his mouth on the white napkin; then he began to talk, and I to listen and to watch his face.

"Bristol has fallen. Prince Rupert saw it was hopeless and surrendered — but there were skirmishes and Stefan was killed."

I was silent, thinking of the last time I had seen Stefan. Poor Stefan: he had asked so little of me and I had given him nothing. I had done what was right, but would it not have been kinder to have given him a little happiness? You see, even when I try to do right I am wrong. The truth is I am a curse on all who look at me with love or desire. But Geraint was speaking again and I brought my wandering thoughts back to the present.

"The King grows desperate, Jalinda. We needed to hold Bristol, and he feels the Prince betrayed his trust. And now the Marquis of Winchester is under siege at Basing House; if that falls too . . . " He shrugged his shoulders in a gesture of defeat.

"His Majesty must be sorely troubled," I said.

"We are urging him to join the Queen in France. It is his only chance — then perhaps we can gather an army with the French king's support and return to fight again in the spring."

"Will he go?" I asked.

Geraint shook his head. "I do not know, Jalinda — I wish I did."

We looked at each other, our faces grave, and I felt that in our shared grief we were closer than we had ever been. Knowing the King as I did, and his deep belief in his divine right to rule, I doubted that he would quit his kingdom for an instant. He believed the rebels must see their duty in the end, no matter if he was defeated in battle. From Geraint's worried look I saw that he thought much as I did. We sat in hopeless silence, thinking bitterly of all our brave plans at the start of the war.

But I was not thinking only of the King. I was grieving for Stefan; a gentle, peaceful man who should never have been a soldier. Of Justin, who was, I knew not where. And of all the other brave, young men who had given their lives in this wicked war between people of the same nation. But most of all, I was thinking of Geraint; of how tired and defeated he looked — and of how much he had come to mean to me.

Thérèse came down to join us then, and Geraint began to talk of other things, regaling us with the latest gossip from the court. It seemed that though the war was desperate, there were still plenty of intrigues and scandal, even if I did guess that he embroidered his tales to make them more exciting for us. He described the latest fashions from France, and I smiled to see Thérèse's pleasure. My eyes met Geraint's and I saw he was laughing in his old, half-mocking way; and I remembered that he had looked at me like that — oh, so many years ago.

So much had happened in the intervening years that it seemed a lifetime away. Surely that young and eager girl had been someone else? A girl with all her life before her, who had not yet begun to hurt and destroy all those she loved. How I wished I could go back to that night and begin again!

Geraint was staring at me strangely, and I am sure he had guessed my thoughts. I blushed, turning away quickly. It was too late for regrets and I would not have him think otherwise.

The next day we told Thérèse that Stefan was dead. She looked blindly at Geraint, her eyes dull and her face ashen. Then she began to scream hysterically and claw at her hair. I moved swiftly, slapping her sharply across the face. Geraint stared at me as she collapsed in my arms, weeping bitterly.

"Oh, Jalinda, Jalinda," she sobbed. "Help me, please help me."

"Hush, my love," I said, stroking her hair. "I shall take care of you, always."

"You won't leave me — you promise you won't leave me!"

"Never while we both live, Thérèse," I said gently. "I will look after you and little Stefan, I promise."

She was still crying, but the hysterical fear had gone, and keeping my arm about her, I drew her towards the stairs. "Now, Thérèse, I am going to put you to bed and give you something to make you sleep. In the morning we shall talk and it won't seem so bad."

"If you say so," she said, clinging to me.

I took her up to her room and sat with her until she fell asleep; then I went back to Geraint. He was pacing about the room, anxiously waiting for me. He began to apologise as soon as he saw me.

"I am sorry, Jalinda. I should have let you decide when to tell her. I had no idea she would be like that . . . "

"How could you know? It was your right to tell her yourself. Thérèse has been living in fear of this so long that it may even be a relief to her now it has happened. Yes, she may even improve now there is nothing to fear . . . "

"Jalinda!" Geraint was shocked.

I looked at him. "Oh, Geraint, I was thinking aloud! I had forgotten for a moment that he was your brother, too. Forgive me . . . "

He looked a little hurt but then he smiled at me. "I was right, Jalinda, you are strong. Stefan could not have done better than to bring her to you."

"So you really did tell him that! I thought Thérèse must have misheard."

"Why — did you imagine I would deny you the qualities I know you to have?"

I shook my head, smiling wryly. "No — you were always honest with me, Geraint. I knew just what you thought of me."

I put my hand to my throat to touch the jade heart, but it was not there: I had given it to Father Renard. Geraint noticed my action and frowned; then he reached inside his doublet and took something out.

"Is this what you seek?" he asked.

I saw the jade heart lying in the palm of his hand and I reached out for it eagerly, but he closed his fingers over it.

"You have seen Father Renard? Why did you not tell me before? Is he well — is he safe?"

He smiled in a way that made my

heart leap for pure joy. "He is well and when I saw him he was on a ship bound for France. I was waiting for you to tell me, Jalinda."

"Waiting for me to tell you — what?" I asked, trembling as I wondered what he would reply.

"About the Roundheads' visit. Father Renard told me you saved everyone's life by meeting them alone and making some bargain with their captain."

I turned away from the glow in his eyes. "He exaggerated, Geraint. I merely gave them my stores. I knew them to be god-fearing men — so where was the danger?"

"If you believed that — why did you hide Father Renard? It was bravely done, Jalinda."

"Nonsense! It is not their way to make war on women. I was perfectly safe."

I tried to take my pendant from him, but still he held it back.

"Father Renard said you saved his life again three days later, making some

239

new bargain with their leader . . . " He looked at me intently and I lowered my eyes. I could not face him. "He said you gave him this pendant, your most precious possession, and he asked me to give it back to you when we met again."

"I am glad to have it back," I said, keeping my face averted. "It is my only ornament since I gave all my jewels to the King . . . "

"Why, Jalinda — why did you save only this?" he asked, and at last I found the courage to look at him.

His dark eyes were glowing with something more than mere approval. My heart leapt joyfully and for a moment I was tempted to tell him what he wanted to hear. Then the memories came flooding back, filling me with shame; and I knew I could not speak, now or ever. I had no right to take the love he was offering me. It was what I wanted most in all the world, but I knew it was impossible — there was too much between us.

He thought he loved me, but how would he feel if he knew what I had given for the priest's life? Would he still think me fine and good if I told him that I had actually taken pleasure in lying in the arms of one of his sworn enemies? He had forgiven one sin, but I was steeped in them; and even if he could forgive, I could not. I was not worthy of such a man: I should stain his honour and ruin him. I knew I must end it finally, for his sake. Then, and only then, would he be free of the curse that was me!

I tossed my head, smiling up at him mockingly. "Why, Geraint — did you think I had kept it in memory of you?" I laughed softly, taking it from him. "Oh, no, my poor friend, I kept it because I did not think the King would want it. I gave him my diamonds and pearls, which Justin bought me, they were more valuable and therefore more fitting for His Majesty."

"Jalinda!" It was a cry from the heart and I knew I had hurt him badly as

I intended. It was hard to go on but I did.

"Of course, it is pretty — and I am glad to have it now."

"God! — I didn't think even you could be this cruel!"

"Oh — but you did, Geraint. You thought my heart harder than this green jade, didn't you? Well — now you see that you were right!" I smiled, though my heart of stone was bleeding.

He looked bewildered and hurt. "I was angry when I wrote that, Jalinda. I was sorry afterwards. Forgive me if I hurt you — and believe that I suffered more."

"Hurt me?" I asked, scorn in every line of my face. "Since you mean nothing to me — except as Justin's cousin — how could you hurt me?"

I saw him flinch and his eyes darkened with pain. In my heart I begged him to forgive me, though I continued to mock him with my eyes.

"If I mean nothing to you — how is it you have been so pleased to see me that you have not asked about Justin once?"

"I heard you tell Thérèse," I said, not meeting his eyes. "Besides, I had a letter from him just before you came."

He studied my face and I knew he thought I was lying, as I was, but he could not prove it.

"You may give him my love, Geraint," I said, smiling, "and tell him I am eager to see him."

"Tell him yourself!" he said, and flung angrily out of the room, slamming the door behind him.

I stared at it through a mist of unshed tears, and I felt my heart breaking, piece by piece. He would never forgive me now! I wanted to scream and cry, but I could not. It was done. My scorn for his gift, which was more precious to me than all the diamonds in the world, and my avowed intention of continuing as Justin's wife, would make his love turn to hate. Now he would forget me and find someone else. It was what I wanted — but why did it hurt so much?

Geraint did not come down for dinner that night, so I dined alone. The next day he left early, with a fond farewell for Thérèse and young Stefan, and a cold stare for me. I held out my hand, bidding him, "God-speed," as if nothing had happened between us. He touched my fingers slightly and turned to leave. Then suddenly he swung back and pulled me roughly into his arms, kissing me fiercely. Taken by surprise, I clung to him as the longing swept over me; then sanity returned and I struggled to free myself. He let me go, looking at me in triumph even as I gathered all my strength for the blow. I struck him across the face with all the force that was in me.

"How dare you?" I cried. "I hate you, Geraint. Do you hear me? I hate you!"

He went white and his hands clenched. For a moment I thought he would kill me and I was glad; then he turned and walked away without another word. The earth spun round. I thought I should faint and a vile sickness swept up through my body. I stared after him as he mounted his horse, longing to call him back. Instead, I went up to the house and let him go.

Thérèse ran after me. She was crying. "Oh, Jalinda — that Geraint should do such a thing! It was wicked of him — I shall never speak to him again!"

"Don't blame Geraint," I said wearily. "It is my fault, not his. I make people unhappy . . . "

"I am angry with him and I shall tell him so when I write. As for you hurting people — I don't believe it. You are so good . . . "

I shook my head. "Remember, Thérèse, you didn't like me once. Remember Selina and what I did to her."

She faltered a little, then: "Oh, that was a long time ago when I was only a silly child. And — and Justin liked you more than Selina, that's all. Besides, she was like me and I do not think she would have enjoyed being married any more than I did. I hated it — it was a relief to come here to you."

I stared at her in disbelief. I had known she was not as much inclined to the intimate side of marriage as I, but I had no idea she felt so strongly. I could not believe that the woman who had screamed so hysterically only yesterday could stand there and calmly tell me that she had never wanted her husband's love. Already she had begun to forget him. She had been fond of him in her way, but he had not touched her heart — poor Stefan.

I could not forget as easily as Thérèse, and Geraint was often in my mind in the months which followed. His visit had shown me how much I loved him and I faced the truth at last. My love for Justin had been a childish hero-worship. I had never really known him at all, and even if our marriage had not been sinful, I believe I should have tired of him in time. He was too weak to have held my respect for long — poor Justin.

★ ★ ★

Once again fate came to my aid, drawing me out of my self-pity and remorse. The weather had been bad all summer and the crops were poor. When the threshing was over it was clear that this was the worst harvest we had known — just when we needed a good one. But I had faced the prospect of a hard winter before and I knew what to do.

I began to set traps for hares and rabbits, and I went out gathering the food which grew wild in the hedgerows and woods. We should not starve; we would just have to change our ways a little.

It was now that I found an ally in Mrs. Beeson. Since Stefan's birth she had grown warmer towards me, and she often joined me on my foraging trips. She was quick and strong and she soon learned what to look for.

The winter passed and it was spring again. The first fresh green shoots of barley poking their heads through the red earth was a heartening sight, and life began to seem good again. Then, just as we were starting to recover from the long winter, we heard terrible rumours.

It was said that there had been a great battle, and that the Royalists had been defeated. At first we feared that the King had been wounded, then we heard that he was dead. We were shocked and grief-stricken, but the stories went on, changing day by day; and then we learnt that His Majesty was still alive and had escaped to Scotland.

The war was over. As we listened to the words, Thérèse and I could hardly believe it. We embraced each other, laughing and crying at the same time. I turned to Ben, who had brought the news, asking him to repeat it.

"'Tis true, mistress," he said, grinning at me. "The war is ended and they say there is to be an agreement betwixt the King and Parliament . . ."

"Then it is truly over . . ."

"And Justin will come home," cried Thérèse. "Oh, Jalinda — just think . . ." She blushed as she met my eyes.

"Yes," I said. "If he is alive."

I wondered what would happen if he returned, and I made up my mind to leave Hallows when he came home.

But the months passed and he did not return, nor was there any sign of a letter to say that he was still alive. The settlement between the King and Parliament did not go well; they wanted him to give assurances and to curtail the limits of his power. He refused. Then we heard that the Scots had betrayed him to his enemies, but he escaped once more. In all nearly a year had slipped by since the battle which destroyed our hopes.

Thérèse continued to look for Justin's return, though I did not believe he would come until the King had regained his throne. But his sister never ceased to look for him; and, one day, hearing the sound of flying hooves, she glanced out of the window and gave a cry of joy. "It is Justin" she said, running down the stairs.

I followed her more slowly, my heart thumping madly. But though the horseman was tall and fair, he was not Justin, only a neighbour come to tell us that the King had raised a new army and was marching south. We were at war again.

Thérèse was in tears, disappointment and fear in her eyes. "Jalinda — not again," she sobbed.

"This time the King will win" I said, praying that I was right.

But this war did not last long and it ended in a shattering defeat for His Majesty. This time the news was bad: the King was taken prisoner, and we who loved him were near to despair.

But surely now the talking would begin, they would settle their differences by debate, instead of the sword. This was the hope of many loyal Englishmen, who, like us, were weary of the strife. And among the stories of plots and escapes, was the feeling that there would be an honourable settlement at last.

At Hallows we waited patiently for news. But when it came — nearly seven years after the war had first begun — we were too stunned to take it in. It could not be true! But we were to learn that it was.

The King had refused to listen to his enemies' demands. He would not give up even the smallest part of his power, which he believed he held by divine right. He would not answer his judges, maintaining that they had no right to try him. And so they took that proud, gracious man, and they cut off his noble head before a crowd of people who had once called themselves his loyal subjects.

They say that as the axe descended a hush fell over the watchers and a great, terrible sigh rose from every throat as though they realised the horror of what had been done in their name. They say it drove terror into the hearts of all who were there — and I hope with all my heart that it was so! For they are surely damned!

England staggered beneath the blow she had dealt herself; and only now did her people begin to know what they had done. For nigh on ten years it was to be a joyless, unhappy land; the Puritans had their hands upon the reins and we were all to know the measure of the men we had allowed to kill our King. It would cost us dearly — and I no less than any other of my countrymen.

It began at once. We received notice that Hallows had been sequestered and was now the property of Parliament. We were permitted to stay in the house until it was decided what was to become of us. I raged inwardly and outwardly. How dare they tell me what I could do in my own house?!

"They cannot do this!" I cried, angrily striding about the room, while Thérèse watched me.

"What can we do?" she asked. "If only Justin was here!"

"Well, he isn't!" I snapped. "I will not be told how to run my estate by these — these petty officials. I shall go to London and complain!"

"You can't — how can you, Jalinda? Will they listen to a woman?"

"I shall make them listen."

She regarded me doubtfully. "Don't go," she said. "What would we do if — if anything happened to you?"

"It won't — but if I should not return, then you must write to Geraint. He will look after you."

She nodded. "Very well, Jalinda — but I wish you would not go . . . "

For once I ignored her pleading. I took Ben with me and made the long journey to Town. It was thus I saw the waste and desolation of the countryside. Houses burnt to the ground, fields bare, ditches choked with weeds — but worst of all were the weary faces of the men we saw along the roadsides, straggling back to their homes. Sometimes alone, sometimes in small bands, often maimed and crippled. Looking into their hopeless eyes, I saw the futility of war as never before; and I found myself searching their faces as we passed by, but Justin was not amongst them.

When we reached London I took two rooms in a hostelry. They were shabby — I could not afford better — but at least the innkeeper was respectable and the sheets were clean. We stayed there two months, though much good it did us. I should have listened to Thérèse.

I petitioned the courts, wrote letters to those in authority, waylaid officials. I begged, pleaded and threatened, but to no avail. I was told my case would be dealt with in due course and coldly reminded that I was the wife of a traitor. At this I flew into a rage and told them just who the traitors were, but I was warned that if I abused the name of those who were now our lawful masters I should be arrested.

At last I realised it was hopeless. I returned home, bitter and defeated. For once in my life my beauty had brought me nothing but scornful looks from these stern men. I had been luckier than I knew when fate sent Robert Francis to Hallows.

* * *

So I returned home to wait for what fate had in store for us next, and for a while our life continued much as it always had. I sometimes wondered if Justin would come back, now that the war was over; but the months passed and we did not hear from him. I began to think that he was either dead or in France.

Thérèse received a letter from Geraint. She brought it to me. "He wants us all to go to him and live in France," she said. "He has offered us a home with him, Jalinda."

I stared at a point just above her head. "You go," I said, "take Stefan with you."

"What about you?"

"I cannot come with you."

"Then I shall not go."

I looked at her. "You must go, Thérèse, it will be better for you in France. It will be hard if they turn us out of Hallows."

"I want to stay with you, Jalinda. I shall tell Geraint so."

I shrugged my shoulders. "As you wish — you can always go later on if you change your mind . . ."

I do not know why I was so stubborn. I had promised Justin I would not go to Geraint, but for all I knew my husband might be dead. No, it was not that promise which held me back, but the knowledge that I would only see hatred in Geraint's eyes. I was too proud to live in his house, knowing that he despised me.

Perhaps I ought to have gone. If I had, then the next tragedy might not have happened, but, since, as usual, I was stubborn, I shall wonder about it until the day I die.

A month later Thérèse caught a chill. It was just a little cold and no one took much notice. She stayed in bed two days and then said she was better.

"Why don't you stay in bed for another day or so?" I asked. "You still look flushed."

She laughed. "Really, Jalinda, you treat me as if I was a child," she said.

"Very well, Thérèse — since you insist, you can unpick this work for me," I replied, more sharply than usual. I was accustomed to her relying on me and resented her small burst of independence. I suppose, in my way, I needed her as much as she needed me.

She looked hurt and I wanted to apologise, but somehow I couldn't find the words.

She came downstairs and sat by the fire, her head bent over the sewing.

But after a while she laid it down and sighed. I didn't say anything; I didn't care whether she did the work or not. I was concerned for her but still a little annoyed. If she wasn't well — why did she have to get up? It was foolish! But as the day wore on her cheeks grew flushed, and by dinnertime she was burning up with a fever. This time I made her go to bed.

The next morning she was still feverish and when I went to her room she clung to my hand, begging me to stay with her. Her skin was red and blotchy, and her hair clung damply to her forehead. I wrung out a cloth in cold water and bathed her face. She smiled at me so sweetly that I wanted to cry.

I sat by her bed all day, talking and bathing her hot body in cool water. I gave her some of Granny's fever mixture, trying all that I knew; but none of it seemed to do any good. I did not know what was wrong with her. She had no rash, no pain, nothing which would give a clue to what ailed her.

In the middle of the night she became delirious, wandering in her mind and sometimes thinking that I was Selina or her father. She called their names, writhing and clawing at the bedcovers. Once she sat up, screaming and pointing to the corner of the room, her eyes wild. I put my arms around her, holding her close to me and stroking her hair until she stopped trembling. Then, just as dawn was breaking, she opened her eyes and looked at me.

"Take care of my son, Jalinda. Promise me you will always take care of him . . ."

"I promise, Thérèse — but you will care for him yourself . . ."

She shook her head and her smile was so gentle that it tore at my heart. "Not this time, dearest Jalinda. You cannot save me this time. But I do not mind — as long as Stefan is with you. I don't want to go on living in this cold, cheerless world. I am tired of this life . . . "

She closed her eyes again, laying back against the pillows. By the time the sun had risen in the sky she was dead. I looked at her still, white face and I longed to weep. If only tears would come, to wash away this bitter pain in my heart. But I could only stare dry-eyed at the girl who was so dear to me now, that we might always have been sisters. The hardships we had endured during the war had drawn us together, and I knew I should miss her desperately.

I closed her eyes, praying her god would take her soul and give it peace. She had not wanted to live now that her world was gone. I did not want to live very much either — but I would.

"Stefan will never forget you, my dear sister," I promised her, as though she could still hear me. "Nor will he forget who and what he is."

It seemed to me then that her face had become calm and she was at peace.

I wrote to Geraint, telling him that Thérèse was dead, and that her last wish had been for me to keep Stefan and bring him up myself. He did not reply to my letter.

★ ★ ★

At this time I came to rely heavily on Ben, for I had little heart for the management of Hallows. I asked him once why he stayed loyal to me, now that I might lose the estate at any time.

He looked at me with those honest eyes of his. "You gave me back my pride, Mistress Frome," he said. "I was nothing until you made me someone. If you asked me for my life I would give it gladly."

I saw that he was sincere, his eyes held no trace of the lust or desire I read in other men's eyes — just a faithful devotion. I felt like weeping but I laughed instead.

"You will do me more good by living

for me, Ben," I said.

He laughed then, riding off about his business, which was also mine. It was the first time I had laughed since my sister died, and one more thing to thank him for.

★ ★ ★

So I worked and waited for the message which would tell me whether I must leave Hallows, or if I was to be permitted to stay. I did not know where Stefan and I would go if we had to leave, but I knew I would manage somehow. Then one day as I was busy in my herb garden I saw a man ride up to the house. He dismounted, wiping the sweat from his brow and walking towards me. For a moment we stared at each other, then he made me a slight bow.

"Good-day, mistress," he said.

"Good-day, sir," I replied.

He did not need to tell me why he had come. It was Robert Francis; he had bought Hallows, as he had always intended to do if the Roundheads won the war — and he had never doubted that they would. Now he had come to claim what was his — but he did not mean only the house and the estate. He had come to claim me, to keep me to the promise I had made so many years before . . .

7

I WORE a grey gown with a white collar when I married Robert Francis, and there were no bridesmaids to lead me by strings tied with rosemary, nor was there a secret blessing in the ruined chapel at Hallows. I cared for none of these things; I was but four and twenty and my heart was dead.

Robert had shown me a paper as proof of Justin's death and I accepted it. I was sad that Justin was dead but I had no more tears left in me.

All that mattered to me now was that I could remain at Hallows and care for Stefan. Stefan, my one reason for living. Robert was a just, if solemn, man. He considered it his duty to allow me to raise my nephew, providing that he was brought up as a Puritan. I agreed but I made my own plans. He should look and act like a little

Puritan, but when he was old enough I would tell him of his mother's faith. Then, when he came to manhood, he could choose for himself.

* * *

A few months after I married Robert we began to hear strange rumours. There was talk of another war. It was said that the son of Charles the Martyr was to march on England with an army he had raised in Scotland.

Robert grew angry, talking of nothing else for days, and denouncing the traitors who had rallied to Charles Stuart's standard — though there were few Englishmen among them, for most of them had been ruined by the last war and could only pray for his success.

King Charles II was crowned in Scotland and he came south, bringing an army of Highlanders with him. Cromwell went to meet him and they fought at Worcester, but it was a disaster for His Majesty. The Scots had no heart for the fight on English soil; and though the infantry resisted bravely, they looked in vain for Leslie's horse.

When the news of the defeat reached us my heart sank. I had hoped so much that the King would win back his throne and free us from the yoke of the Puritans. However, Robert was delighted and I dare not let him guess my true feelings, though I did ask:

"Would it not be better if the King came back now, Robert? Is it not time to forget old grievances?"

He frowned at me. "Certainly not, wife. The Stuarts have been nothing but a blight on this land — and we want no more of them!"

"But, Robert . . . "

"You are a woman and cannot understand these things. I will hear no more of this treacherous talk!"

I seethed inwardly. He dismissed my arguments arbitrarily, so certain was he that he was right. I bit back my angry retort, for I knew it was useless to argue with him. But I continued to hope that the King would return to England one day.

There were rumours that His Majesty had been taken prisoner and I feared for him; but the stories were false and he escaped to France.

With the defeat at Worcester it seemed that Charles Stuart's hopes were at an end, and my heart ached for that merry child who was now condemned to a life of lonely exile. But perhaps his life was no harder than mine.

The years which followed were to be the unhappiest I had known.

The Puritans were a joyless people. They were very pious and thought it a sin to dance or sing. Our lives must be spent in quiet devotion to God and our brethren. In all honesty I must admit they were just, respectable people, and the Lord Protector Cromwell, a good man according to his principles. But I found England a dull, solemn land beneath his rule.

In time even Cromwell found it impossible to cope with the stubborn men who thought themselves the only judges of what was right for England. In the end he did as the King had done before him; he dismissed Parliament and ruled alone. So what had we gained? We had exchanged a King for a Lord Protector; a gay life for solemn looks and sterner laws. And for this so many had given their lives!

Yet I felt no hatred for Cromwell himself. It was the Puritan preachers with their talk of eternal damnation whom I disliked.

My husband was a lay preacher. He loved nothing more than to thunder and frown down on we poor sinners, forced to listen to his ranting. Perhaps it was because Robert felt himself a sinner that he tried so hard to prove that he was not. He came to my bed, seeking the pleasure he craved, as seldom as he could. He was driven to seek relief in my arms, and forced by his sense of sin to beg forgiveness on his knees.

Sometimes he stayed away from me for weeks, only to come back when his torment became more than he could bear. I pitied him, yet I also despised him, for we could have found a kind of happiness together if he had been able to accept himself for what he was. But he could not and so I was glad when he stayed away; for an hour in his arms meant two on my knees, praying for the salvation of my soul.

He repented and he made me repent, too. It was uncomfortable and boring; but I soon learned to think of other things while he was busy consigning us to hell and the fire for our sins.

I was allowed no ornaments, no scrap of lace or colours in my dress. This annoyed me, but I obeyed him, though I continued to wear the jade heart beneath my gown. One day he saw it and sternly asked me why I wore it when he had forbidden me to wear any jewellery.

I lowered my eyes. "I will remove it if it is your wish, husband," I said.

"But it was my mother's — a good, honest woman. I wear it to remind me that it becomes me to be like her."

I waited breathlessly — would he call me a shameless liar? I need not have worried; it never occurred to Robert that I might be other than I seemed. His frown disappeared.

"Since it was your mother's and you do not wear it for vanity's sake, you may continue to wear it beneath your gown," he said in a pious tone.

"Why, I thank you, husband," I said, my hands clasped meekly before me. "You are surely kind, and I honour you — just as much as you deserve."

He smiled, well pleased with my answer. Poor Robert; he thought I was complimenting him and he found me a very satisfactory wife. He came to my bed that night, and in the morning kept me on my knees for only half an hour. He was truly pleased with me!

It was wrong of me to mock my husband as I did, for he was a just man according to his standards. But

I could not bend my will to his in all things, letting my mind stagnate and decay. He possessed my body and that was all he wanted anyway. I doubt he even knew I had a mind, less cared how it thought or felt. To Robert a woman was a mere chattel for his comfort and ease, so I cheated him of nothing he really cared for. If he had once tried to understand me I might have been more dutiful. But he did not, therefore I considered myself free to act and think as I wished.

Sometimes I wonder why I stayed with him. I could have walked into the sea, but that would have left Stefan to Robert's tender mercies. I could have left my husband and become a harlot; but I might have ended at the cart's tail, being whipped naked through the streets — and what of Stefan then? Or I could have gone to Geraint. But I could not do that, and so I stayed and I did what I had always done best: I cheated and lied to gain my own way.

I soon discovered that, in spite of his pride in himself, my husband was a stupid man. For a start, he could not read. He would not admit it and he refused to let me teach him. After a while I ceased bothering about his ignorance and used it to my advantage.

He had forbidden me to read anything but the Bible he had given me, and I was allowed only plain sewing. My pretty threads and tapestries must all be destroyed. I hid them, working on them only when I knew he was safely gone for the day; and I took the cover from his Bible, using it to hide books of a similar shape and size. That way I could sit reading a play right under my pious husband's nose.

One day he saw me smiling as I read, and he frowned in sudden suspicion. "Read me something from the Bible, wife," he said.

"Certainly, Robert," I replied, and repeated several passages which I had memorised.

He nodded, smiling coldly. He was

proud of his dutiful wife, who took so much pleasure in reading the Bible. In fact he was so proud of me that he boasted to his friends of my piousness.

Several of them came to call on us soon after; they asked if I would read the lesson in church the following Sunday, as an example to the other women. It was an honour seldom bestowed on a woman; however, I refused. I would mock them and their pious ways; I would not mock God — if he existed.

"Forgive me, good sirs," I said, veiling my eyes with my long lashes. "But I am only a woman and therefore a creature of sin. I am not worthy to read aloud in God's House."

I knew this to be their belief; they could not deny the truth of my words.

"Mistress Francis, I honour you for your true modesty. We shall not press you again."

One of the elders spoke and I gave him a meek, yet grateful smile. However, Robert protested, urging me to do as I was asked.

"Your wife speaks wisely, Robert Francis," the elder said. "She is a truly modest woman and a fitting wife for you, sir. It must be for you to give the lesson instead."

Robert was silenced: there was nothing he liked more than to be given a chance to deliver yet another of his fiery sermons.

So I had tricked him once more.

It was the same with Stefan. As he grew to adolescence I began to instruct him in simple Latin and the faith which had comforted his mother.

"This is our secret, Stefan," I told him. "You must never tell Robert."

He promised solemnly, his blue eyes wide and scared. Poor child; he was terrified of my husband and crept about like a mouse when he was home, which suited Robert, since he believed a child should always be quiet and obedient. But when we were alone, we laughed and played silly games together.

He spent a great deal of his time in the kitchen with Mrs. Beeson and I did not forbid him. I knew he was safe with her, because she loved him, too.

So between us we deceived Robert and I do not regret it. If he had been more tolerant it would not have been necessary. But it was the same in many Puritan households, and I doubt I was the only woman to snatch a little pleasure behind her too pious husband's back.

One thing I was sorry for — we did not have a child. Perhaps if Robert could have held his own son in his arms his heart might have been touched with tenderness at last. It would have been a joy and a comfort to me, too, but it was not to be.

★ ★ ★

The years passed and most of the time I was too busy to dwell on my unhappiness. I learned to live with my husband and I expected nothing from him — or from life.

Then something happened which was to have far-reaching consequences for England, and for me. The Lord Protector died and his son took his place. For a while the country mourned Cromwell's death, but soon there was unrest again. A flare-up of old rivalrys betwixt the diehard Puritans and those who, like me, preferred a less strict way of life. Richard Cromwell was not the man his father had been; weak, ineffectual, he was unable to control an ungrateful Parliament. Now the voices began to murmur that it was time to recall the King, but his enemies opposed any move in this direction.

Then a new man came forward. He was a soldier, who had once been a Royalist, but later served the Commonwealth's cause in Ireland, Scotland and at sea, against the Dutch. His name was General Monk, a name respected by both sides. He was convinced that England's troubles could only be settled by the King's return, and to that end, he marched on England from Scotland. He was unopposed and he recalled the Long Parliament so that a general election could be held. The new government invited Charles Stuart to return — but there were to be limits to his power.

The people had spoken. England was tired of the solemn Puritans and their eternal preaching. Now we waited with bated breath — would the King accept these restrictions? Or would he prove as stubborn as his father?

The second King Charles had learned to bend, to give a little. He accepted Parliament's terms; he came home and he was crowned King of England.

The whole country went mad with delight. The maypoles were brought out and people danced in the streets. They laughed, they drank, they brawled and they wenched. They welcomed the King with open arms — and forgot that they had done the same for Cromwell! In fact, hardly a man in the country could be brought to admit he had ever been anything but a king's man — a circumstance which did not escape His Majesty's sharp wit.

"It seems to be my own fault that I have been so long absent," he remarked with a wry smile to one of his gentlemen, "since everybody I see protests that he has always wished for my return."

I know not what that gentleman replied, but I will wager he laughed right merrily, for the King was home and all who truly loved him were satisfied at last.

Women burned their grey gowns and brought out all their finery. It was a time of celebration and joy — except at Hallows. Robert Francis was not a man to change his mind simply because the rest of England did so. I did put on a red dress on the day of His Majesty's return but my husband scowled at me.

"What is that, woman?" he asked. "Have you forgot yourself?"

I begged his pardon and went to

change it. I saw no sense in annoying him merely for vanity's sake, though my heart was at the point of rebellion. Was there to be no end to this dreary purgatory? For a while it seemed that things would go on as they were; then everything changed.

I was in the garden. It was warm, a pleasant breeze just ruffling the treetops as I worked in my herb garden. I wiped a trickle of sweat from my brow, straightening up to ease my aching back. As I did so my eye was drawn to a horseman approaching the house. I could tell he was a Royalist, from his fine clothes and the plumes in his hat.

I watched him draw nearer, something telling me who it was even before I could see his fair hair, curled in a neat lovelock, and his small, pointed beard. When I had last seen him he had been clean-shaven, yet I knew him at once. My mouth felt dry and my knees turned to water as he dismounted and came to me. He was as handsome as ever, his eyes as blue as the summer sky. He looked at me and our eyes locked in an agony of heart-tearing emotion.

"Hello, Jalinda," he said.

"Justin . . . " I whispered. "I thought you were dead."

His mouth twisted into a parody of a smile. "Oh, no, my loving wife. I am very much alive, as you will shortly see . . . "

I stared at him silently. Nothing I could say would change a thing, no words ease his festering hurt.

"You had best come up to the house," I managed, after what seemed an eternity.

His eyes were cold and bitter as he looked at me. I drew in my breath sharply, then I gathered up my skirts and ran back to the house. Justin followed me purposefully. It was the wrong thing to do — but when did I ever do right? I should have reasoned with him, sent him away, anything . . . But would he have gone? I doubt it. He had come to claim what was his — Hallows — and me.

I thought, hoped, that he and Robert would be sensible about the house and estate. As for me, I could not live as Justin's wife, and I did not want to go on living with Robert. Perhaps Justin would let me have Stefan — if not, then I must leave the boy with his uncle and go away by myself.

How foolish I was to think it could all be solved so easily. They fought, of course, though I begged and pleaded with them. They both ignored me. Their faces were hard, their eyes full of a bitter hatred which was beyond all reason. I ran between them, pushing them apart, pleading with them to listen.

"Stay out of this, Jalinda — I'll deal with you later!" said Justin, thrusting me to one side.

"Be quiet, wife, this is men's business!" — this from the Puritan.

They glared at each other furiously.

"My wife." Justin was dangerously

calm. "Your whore."

"Nay, I married her in good faith. You sent no word all these years — she is more my wife than yours."

"By God! — I'll see you dead for that!"

"You may try, you traitorous popinjay . . ."

I watched in mounting exasperation. "Cease your wrangling," I cried. "I'll be wife to neither of you any more — so do not waste your breath in arguing over me!"

"You talk foolishly, wife," said Robert, glancing at me coldly. "You will do as I bid you."

"I told you once, Jalinda — I would rather see you dead than in another man's arms. You should have believed me . . ."

I stared at them hopelessly, knowing that I could do nothing to prevent them from trying to kill each other. I was only a part of it. The war, Hallows, old hatreds, pride — all these things combined to make it inevitable.

Yet I should have done something. I ought to have fetched help, screamed, prayed, wept — anything! — to make them stop; but I could only watch, transfixed by a horrible fascination that held me fast.

They moved around each other, swords drawn, eyes locked in silent conflict. Then their blades crossed in a flurry of blows, the noise echoing in the lofty room. I put my hands to my ears, trying to blot out the sound of their breathing; heavy, violent, terrifying. I wanted to turn away so that I should not have to watch, but I could not move. I was forced to follow every action, feel every blow, as the fight went first one way, then the other.

Robert was a big man and strong. He pressed down hard on Justin, and I thought his very strength must win the day. However, as I watched, I saw they were evenly matched; for, though Robert was strong, he was not intelligent. Justin was lighter on his feet and he had a quick, able mind.

He outwitted Robert time and time again, making him thrust clumsily, parrying the blade and twisting it aside with careless ease. I saw that there could be only one end — Justin must win. He was toying with Robert, deliberately baiting him, making him lose his temper so that his thrusts became even wilder. Justin was smiling, a cruel, horrible smile that made me shiver. He was slowly wearing Robert down; he knew it and he relished his superiority over the older man.

The end came suddenly. Robert realised that Justin was the better swordsman; he was tiring, his legs beginning to feel heavy and his breath coming in harsh gasps. He had to finish it soon and he threw himself into the attack, hoping to take his opponent by surprise. The fury of his blows forced Justin back, causing him to stumble against a chair. Robert thought he saw his chance and he stabbed at his opponent's heart, but Justin wrenched aside so that the blade tore harmlessly through his sleeve. Robert brought his sword up sharply, but Justin had recovered his balance and he spun his sword, parrying the blow deftly, before driving his own blade deep into Robert's side. The blood spurted out in a fountain of crimson, as the older man's face stiffened in a look of startled horror and he sank to the ground.

I gasped, thinking he was dead and sickened by the sight of the blood; but I was still held motionless by that strange force which bound my limbs. Justin turned to look at me, and I saw the insane glee in his eyes as through the purple haze of a nightmare. He came towards me, his feverish eyes exploring my face as if he was trying to absorb every detail before it was too late. I knew, even as he spoke, what he meant to do.

"And now for you, my love," he said, the light of madness in his eyes. "I cannot forget you. I cannot live with you — and I do not want to live without you. You must die, and

I will follow you to the grave. You will not be alone for long, Jalinda, for we shall lie side by side for all eternity."

My head was spinning as I gazed up at the man I had once loved so desperately, a man who was a stranger now. I wanted to cry out, to beg him to think of Stefan, but I could not speak. And somewhere in my secret soul, I was thinking: "Yes, this is right — this is how it must end. I deserve to die." Geraint would come for Stefan, I knew. "Geraint, Geraint, my love, forgive me. Forgive me, Selina, forgive me, Father . . . "

Justin was so close to me, his face white, clasping his bloodied sword. He raised it to strike, then groaned. "I loved you," he whispered hoarsely, "more than my eternal soul. One kiss, one last kiss before you die . . . "

He drew me to him, his face working in an agony of pain and desire. I could feel the pent-up force of his emotion as his body shook and his lips fastened on mine hungrily. I closed my eyes, going limp in his arms.

It was then that Robert struck. He had managed to crawl to his sword and with the last remnants of his strength he climbed to his feet. I opened my eyes just as he raised his arm to strike, and I struggled, trying to warn Justin; but he held me tightly, his mouth still bruising mine as Robert plunged the blade into his back. Justin's head jerked back and he fell forward against me. I caught him in my arms, sinking to the ground beneath his weight and cradling him to my breast. He looked up at me and I saw that the insane hatred had gone. His eyes were gentle, loving, kind — just as they had always been in the past.

"Oh, Jalinda," he breathed. "I loved you so. Why were we so cursed, my beloved?"

"I don't know, Justin, I don't know," I said, and the tears I had thought long dried came then. "I loved you, too. I love you still."

It was true. I loved him as my brother and the friend he had once been. The hot, scalding tears ran from my eyes, spilling on to his face. He smiled. It was such a gentle, tender smile, that it stabbed my heart with remorse.

"You are so beautiful when you cry, Jalinda — so beautiful. Forgive me, my love . . . "

He closed his eyes and the rattle of death was in his throat. A trickle of blood oozed from the corner of his mouth as I bent to kiss his lips and tasted the warm stickiness of his heart's blood. I held him closer, rocking back and forth in my agony and sobbing bitterly. At that moment it seemed to me that I gazed into the bottomless pit of hell itself.

"Forgive me, Justin," I begged him, my tears falling on to his still face. "Forgive me . . . "

But he could not answer me, for he was dead. He was dead because I had ruined his life and brought him to this wretched end. I was his murderer and I wished that I could die, too. I sat there, holding his lifeless body until they came and took him from me. I fought wildly then, screaming like a madwoman and clinging to him with all my strength; but they tore my hands from him and led me away — Mrs. Beeson and Ben, my only friends.

Later they told me that Robert was dead, too. But what did I care for that? I had made a bargain with him and I had paid in full. I should not grieve for Robert Francis, but I would weep for all those I had destroyed. In the lonely hours of the night I would remember and I would weep. I should think too of the man I loved. The man to whom I could never go — even though I was free. I was free at last, but freedom would not wash away my guilt, nor did I want to be absolved. I had deserved my punishment and I would accept it.

8

I KNOW not how I lived through the first few days after Justin's death. I was nearly mad with grief and remorse. I had loved him so deeply once and, despite all that lay between us, I loved him still. No matter that the nature of my love had changed, no matter that I also loved Geraint — a part of me would always belong to Justin.

I could not forget the horror of his death. Each night I spent endless hours restlessly pacing the narrow passages. The house seemed to mock at me, taunting me with echoes of the past so that I thought I heard the voices of those who had lived within its walls. Sometimes I would see shadowy figures waiting in dark corners; they beckoned to me, smiling and whispering. But when I ran towards them they were gone.

"Come back — please, come back!" I begged. "I am so alone . . . "

But they could not come back — they were dead, all dead.

For weeks I cared not how I looked or what I ate — or if I ate at all. I even avoided my dear Stefan, for to look at him brought back memories too painful to be borne. I began to ride out beyond the boundaries of the estate, to walk across the cliffs and windswept beaches, returning late at night and drenched to the skin. Ben watched me anxiously and I was vaguely aware that he was worried by my long, lonely treks. But my thoughts were only for those who no longer walked or breathed or lived. I was totally immersed in my private pain; this hell which haunted my every moment, whether waking or sleeping.

Then one day, some two months after Justin's death, I found myself near Granny's cottage. I halted, staring at it and wondering what had brought me here after all these years. I tried to turn away, but something drew me towards the door. I pushed it open, and it swung back, falling drunkenly on its broken hinges.

The roof had gaping holes, and parts of the walls had begun to cave in. As my eyes became accustomed to the gloom I saw that much of the decay was the result of wanton destruction. Granny's few possessions had been smashed, to lie forgotten and desolate among the dust. Something caught my eye and I bent down to pick it up. It was the wooden horse carved so lovingly for me all those years ago; but someone had broken the legs and snapped off the head. It was a small thing compared with all the rest, but somehow I found it unbearable. I dropped the toy, covering my face with my hands as the scalding tears broke from me.

"Granny, oh, Granny — what can I do?" I wept.

"'Tis no use grieving for them as have gone, Jalinda. We must think of the living."

Were the words only in my head, or did she really speak to me from beyond the grave? I cannot tell. I only know I was comforted. Deep in my heart I knew she was right. I had been neglecting Stefan and the estate; it was time to put my grief behind me.

I left the cottage and turned towards Hallows. The threads of my life must be picked up again. I felt the warmth of the sun touch my face, and breathed deeply. Then I had a curious feeling that someone was watching me. Watching me with an intensity which had communicated itself to me.

I turned and saw him standing at the top of the cliffs; a tall, dark man, outlined against the blue sky. The sun was in my eyes, blinding me so that his face was indistinct, but I knew that it would be full of hatred. I could sense the anger in him and I shivered, cold despite the warm sunshine. A strange foreboding crept over me, turning me to stone as our eyes met in silent conflict. When I could bear it no longer I tore my eyes from his, forcing myself to walk away; then, all at once, I was running, fleeing back down the hill to Hallows and safety, driven by a terrible fear that he desired my death.

I stumbled over the rough ground, trembling with fright. My hair had come tumbling down my back and my gown was torn where it caught on a briar bush in my mad flight. Even when I reached the house I did not feel safe until the heavy lock was turned behind me. Pouring wine into a glass, I gulped it down, choking as it stung my dry throat.

It was like one of the nightmares which still awoke me at times and it filled me with a nameless terror. But after a while I stopped shaking and began to laugh. How stupid of me to start at shadows, letting my imagination run wild. It was my morbid curiosity and the desolation of Granny's cottage. I had allowed my fancies to cloud my mind, which was not really surprising after the way I had been living these past weeks. The wonder was that I was not entirely mad!

Just because a stranger stared at me I had lost my head. And even if he had meant me harm — what did it matter? Had I not been longing for death? I realised with a small shock that I wanted to live. That deep instinct for survival was as strong as ever, and I knew that whatever blows life had to offer, I would go on.

I must think of Stefan now. He was almost a young man; intelligent, sensitive, with an inquiring mind, he needed someone to teach him the things his father would want him to know. He needed the companionship of other boys, too, something neither I or Mrs. Beeson could supply. Because of her he had not suffered from my neglect these past weeks, but I knew I must put aside my selfish grief. I tidied my hair, smoothed my gown and went to find Mrs. Beeson.

She smiled at me as I entered the kitchen and I think she knew that I had put my sorrow behind me.

"I have come to thank you," I said.

She nodded, understanding at once. "'Twas nothing, mistress. I but did my duty as you have ever done yours." She looked at me, a deep sadness in her eyes. "I was wrong about you," she said at last.

"Wrong — in what way?"

"I thought you trouble from the start," she said frowning, "a curse upon this house."

"And so I was — I am!"

She shook her head. "Nay, lass. Methinks you bring trouble on yourself and others, but 'tis not in you. You bring suffering to those who love you — but you suffer more than they . . . "

I could feel the hot sting of tears in my eyes, but I could not speak. I stared at her, struggling to hold back the surge of emotion in my heart.

She smiled at me. "I pray for you, Jalinda. I pray that God will show you the way to peace and happiness."

"Thank you," I whispered. Then

I fled before I disgraced myself by weeping in her arms.

★ ★ ★

The weather had been very hot all summer, each successive day seeming hotter than the last. I could not remember a year quite like this. Ponds began to dry up and the stream in the village dwindled to a mere trickle. But at Hallows we were fortunate, for our spring continued to bubble to the surface despite the lack of rain.

I told Ben to let the villagers use our water. Some of them came, most did not; but it never occurred to me to question their absence too closely. It was a fair distance to walk and I supposed them to have found a supply nearer their homes. Besides, I had problems of my own.

I had heard that Robert's brother intended to claim the estate. In all the years I was married to Robert I met his brother only three times, and that was more than enough. I disliked him intensely and I had no intention of remaining at Hallows as his dependant.

So, as I seldom went down to the village, I had no idea of what was happening; perhaps I should never have known if the tragedy had not struck closer to home. The first I knew of the troubles was when Ben rode up to the house one morning and sat waiting outside. I went to meet him, surprised that he had not come in as he usually did. He cried out as he saw me:

"Come no nearer, mistress!"

"Why — what is it, Ben?"

"There is pox in the village — and I fear Bessie has taken it."

His voice faltered as he spoke and I looked at him with sympathy; for Bessie was his youngest sister and I knew how much he loved her. It took me only seconds to make my decision: Ben had done so much for me, now I would repay him if I could.

"Go home, Ben, and tell your mother

to prepare to leave the cottage. I will follow as quickly as possible."

He stared at me. "Leave the cottage . . . ?" A look of fear crossed his face. "You'll not turn us out, mistress?"

"Of course not!" I frowned impatiently. "But you must leave for a while — you can move into one of the barns with your family — so that I can nurse Bessie."

"Nurse Bessie? Nay, I cannot allow . . . "

"You must trust me, Ben. There is a chance that I can save Bessie, but I cannot care for all of you, so you must leave lest you take it from her. Do you trust me?"

He stared at me, a red flush creeping up his thick neck. "Aye, mistress, with my life — but I would not have harm come to you . . . "

"There is no risk for me, I promise you. My parents died of the pox but it did not touch me — it will not do so now. Please do as I ask, Ben . . . "

I watched him, seeing his inner struggle. He nodded. "It shall be as you say," he mumbled, then turned and rode back the way he had come. I watched him for a moment before hurrying to the kitchens.

Mrs. Beeson looked alarmed as I told her what was happening. "You cannot do it, Mistress Jalinda," she cried. "You will surely take it yourself!"

"All I ask of you is that you have a care for Stefan. If I should not return, then you must send word to Geraint. I shall not come back until the infection has gone and you must not let Stefan come to me — nor must any of you go near the village."

She nodded. "Aye, trust me for that — but I like not the thought of you all alone in that cottage . . ."

I laughed at her anxious face. "Why — surely you know I am too wicked to die? I shall be safe enough, never fear. Now there are things I need, will you pack them for me while I say farewell to Stefan?"

She sighed. "I dare say you'll go your own way as always. Aye, I'll do as you bid me . . . "

"Thank you," I replied meekly, hiding my smile.

I ran upstairs to find Stefan and tell him I was going away for a while. He looked at me and I knew he did not want me to go, but he only smiled and told me not to worry about him. Once he would have clung to me and cried, but he was too old for tears now, or, at least, he hid them until after I had gone.

When I reached the cottage, Ben's mother was in tears. She did not want to leave her youngest child and she entreated me to let her stay. But I dare not permit it, for the risk of infection was too great, and she had other children who needed her.

"Ben can bring us food each day," I said. "He will give you news of her."

"Don't let my Bessie die," she cried. "She is such a little thing . . . "

"I will care for her as if she were my

own," I promised.

"You must trust me."

Ben put his arm about her and she collapsed against him. "Come away, Mother," he said, his eyes on my face. "The mistress will save her if anyone can."

"Thank you," I whispered, smiling at him as he led her away, still weeping.

Inside, the cottage was dark and stiflingly hot; the window tightly shut and a fire burning in the grate despite the heat of the day. I opened the shutters, grateful for a breath of fresh air; then I went to look at the child. Her face was flushed and she whimpered fretfully.

"Would you like me to bathe your face, Bessie?" I asked.

She nodded, moaning and pulling at the coverlet. I fetched water and gently bathed her burning flesh. She seemed easier for a time, but soon she was tossing restlessly on her cot again. I sat beside her all day and throughout the night, soothing her as best I could.

But by morning the red patches had begun to spread across her face and I knew for certain that she had the dread disease.

When Ben came with the food I would not let him enter. He stood outside, staring at me silently, a single tear running slowly down his cheek.

"Why?" he asked bitterly. "Why Bessie? — she's only a child. She never harmed anyone in her life . . . "

"Don't despair, Ben. Sometimes people recover . . . "

His eyes held a look of hopelessness. "She's only a baby," he repeated.

He turned away, his shoulders hunched, the limp in his walk more noticeable now. I went back to the child. As the day wore on the foul blisters spread over her face and she cried out in pain, trying to claw at the irritation with her nails. I bound her hands in clean linen; then I smoothed a cooling balm over her flesh. It seemed to ease her a little, as did the mixture I spooned into her mouth; but nothing helped very much.

For twelve days and nights — or was it more? — I kept a vigil at her side. I cannot be sure how long I sat there, watching her desperate struggle for life; time ran into itself in an endless blur of pain and sleepless nights. I was afraid to turn my eyes from her, lest she slip away from me. I was weary and near to defeat, yet I refused to admit that she could die. I used every ounce of skill I had and I prayed, too.

I wasn't sure if God existed and I doubted that my prayers would be welcome. But if there really was a God, surely He couldn't want this innocent child to die? Perhaps he listened, or perhaps my nursing was all that was needed, I do not know, but at last the battle was won. There were no new sores and the old ones began to fade. Bessie would have a few scars but she would live. She would live!

I shall never forget the look on Ben's face when I told him the news. For a moment he just stared at me in disbelief; then a look of wonder dawned in his eyes and suddenly he was laughing and crying.

"Tell your mother she can come back now," I said.

He seized my hands, kissing them fervently. "You are an angel," he said. "Thank you, thank you . . ."

I laughed. "I am not an angel, Ben — a witch, perhaps?"

He turned pale, looking over his shoulder fearfully. "Be careful, mistress," he warned. "'Tis not wise to say such things — even in jest."

"I do not think you would want to burn me," I said, smiling.

I spoke lightly and was surprised by the intensity of his reply. "Nay, mistress, I would die before I let harm come to you! But there are others . . ."

I shrugged carelessly. "If they wish to be foolish, then let them. I am tired and I am going home to sleep. Bring your mother back; the infection has gone, but Bessie is still weak and she needs her mother. Make sure she has plenty of milk and butter — take whatever you want from the stores."

He shuffled his feet awkwardly. "You are too good to us, mistress."

"Nonsense! If it were not for you, Ben, I should have nothing to give. I have only repaid a part of all you have done for me."

He shook his head, but I smiled and left him. I went back to Hallows, and after I had washed away the stink of sickness and burnt my clothes, lest they carried the infection, I lay down on my bed. I fell into a deep sleep and when I woke at last it was morning once more. As I sat up, stretching and yawning, Mrs. Beeson entered, bringing me a tray of delicious food.

I smiled. "You will spoil me," I said.

"You look as if you could do with spoiling," she scolded. "You are as thin as a heronshaw! Now you just eat up every scrap of this food, miss!"

It was years since she had spoken

to me in this way and I almost felt a child again. It was a good feeling and I began to eat hungrily. She watched me with a satisfied smile, then went back to her work. For a while I lay where I was, relaxed and happier than I had been for years. Then I threw back the covers, impatient to see Stefan. I dressed quickly and hurried downstairs, but as I reached the hall I saw Mrs. Beeson coming towards me. She looked grim and I felt a stab of fear.

"What is the matter?" I asked, my heart thumping. "It isn't Stefan? He hasn't taken the pox?!"

She shook her head and I breathed more easily. "Nay, 'tis a woman from the village. She is outside in the yard and insists upon seeing you."

"I will go out to her," I said.

The woman looked at me, her eyes dark with fear as I asked her what she wanted of me. "'Tis my son," she said. "He is but six years old . . ."

"Has he taken the pox?"

She nodded. "You saved Ben's

sister — save my child, I beg you."

I looked at her. I did not want to go; I was tired and I wanted to be with Stefan. It was in my mind to refuse, but she held out her hands in supplication, sinking to the ground at my feet and clutching my gown.

"Please, Mistress Frome," she sobbed. "He is all I have . . ."

I sighed. "Will you leave me alone with him?"

"Yes, mistress, anything — only come to him!"

"Very well, I will come. But you must leave your cottage; I cannot nurse you both. Go home and wait for me — but do not touch the boy. It will avail you nothing if I save him and you die."

She thanked me and scurried away. I went up to the kitchen, to find that Mrs. Beeson had packed a basket for me, though her face was set in grim disapproval.

"I suppose you will go," she said. "'Tis beyond all sense, tempting fate twice in a row — and for the likes of them!"

"You know you don't mean a word of that," I said smiling. "Take care of Stefan. I shall not go up to him; it would only upset him."

She sniffed loudly, a suspicion of tears in her eyes. I put down the basket and hugged her, realising in that moment how strong were the ties which bound us; despite our many disagreements.

"Go on with you!" she said gruffly.

I laughed. "I told you once — I am too wicked to die. I shall return to plague you . . . "

"See that you do!"

I picked up my basket and left before I changed my mind. It would be so easy to stay at Hallows and let the village boy take his chances, but I had given my word to his mother. And when I saw the relief in her eyes I was glad that I had not refused her.

I looked at the boy's face; it was already showing signs of the evil pestilence. "The disease has gained a hold on him," I said, "but I will do what I can."

"I ask no more," she replied, then: "I do not know how I shall pay you . . . "

"I want no payment, madam." I smiled at her. "He is young, there is a chance that he will live. But you must go now."

She looked at me strangely; then she crossed herself and ran from the cottage as if she was afraid of something. Well, she had need to fear for her son; the pox was more advanced in him than it had been in Bessie when I went to her. I sighed, it was an almost impossible task but I must do what I could for him.

I looked around the cottage. It was filthy, the rushes matted and greasy beneath my shoes. First I would make the boy as comfortable as possible, then I must do something with this hovel. I longed for Mrs. Beeson's kitchen, with pewter pots so clean they reflected your face; even Ben's cottage had been neat and tidy with fresh rushes on the floor.

This cottage was almost as bare as Granny's had been; suddenly the irony of my situation made me laugh. I felt better at once and began to roll up my long sleeves; there was no sense in wasting time when so much needed to be done.

* * *

Time merged into itself once more and I know not how long I spent alone in that cottage; but at last the day came when the boy's fever broke and the sores faded from his skin, leaving pitted marks which would remain with him for life. He was weak, but at least he was alive. I sent Ben to fetch the child's mother and told her that she must nurse her son now; then I left her house. But this time I did not go back to Hallows. The pox was everywhere in the village. Ben brought me more of the cooling balm and I took it from house to house, explaining what they must do; for there were so many sick and I could not nurse them all.

Ben brought me my horse. He wanted to wait for me but I sent him away. He had problems enough without worrying over me. The harvest still had to be gathered in and, with the sickness in the village, labour was short.

"If you do not return by dusk I shall come for you," he said.

"I have several more cottages to visit. Don't worry — I shall be all right."

He looked anxious, but he was accustomed to obeying me and in the end he rode away. I am not sure when I first realised something was wrong; but gradually a feeling of unease crept over me. Perhaps it was the sullen faces — or perhaps it was just a premonition, I cannot tell.

It was nearly dusk by the time I came out of the last cottage. I untied my horse from the rail and climbed wearily into the saddle. I was tired, terribly tired. My horse moved forward slowly, then halted as my hands slackened on the reins. I closed my eyes for a moment, exhaustion sweeping over me. Then my eyes jerked open as I heard the strange whispering sound. They were all around me, a sea of faces, black with hatred. I could feel the anger flowing from their midst as if it were a physical thing; it enveloped me in a web of fear.

"Let me pass," I said.

One or two moved back, but most stood firm and there was some jostling as the braver among them pushed to the front. It was then that the whispering began to make sense: they had named me for a witch once more.

"Burn the witch — she brought the evil on us!"

"My son died, he was only three. Why should he die while she lives?"

"My pond dried and my cow died of thirst. It has never happened before — 'tis the witch's doing!"

"She brought the sickness on us.

Why does she not sicken and die like the rest of us?" demanded a tall, dark man with piercing eyes. "I'll tell you why, my friends, 'tis because she is a witch!"

"Burn her — burn the witch!"

The cry was on every side, in every throat. It rose to a crescendo, filling my ears, beating in my brain. Their faces reflected the blood-lust which haunted my dreams: like beasts from the fiery furnace.

The man with the penetrating eyes held up his hand for silence. I stared at him as he faced me, his eyes glittering with triumph; and suddenly I knew him. It was the man who had watched me on the cliffs that day, and now I knew why he hated me.

"Aye — you recognise me now, witch," he said. "You cursed my father and he died in agony — with your name on his lips."

I looked into his eyes, knowing that I was doomed. He was the son of my enemy and he would finish what his father had begun all those years ago; this time there was no one to save me. I had sent Ben away. My faithful Ben, who had tried to warn me — but I had not listened and now I should pay for my heedlessness. These people, whom I had never harmed, desired my death, and Justin could not come this time. I smiled a little bitterly. I had tried to help these people, yet they hated me; but those whom I had hurt grievously had never ceased to love me. How strange was life . . .

The tall man watched me, relishing his victory, then he turned to the crowd. "What shall we do with the witch?" he cried.

"Burn her, burn her, burn her!" the cry rang out again.

He smiled at me, a cruel, chilling look. "Take her, take the witch!"

Their hands reached for me, pulling at my gown, trying to drag me from my horse. For a moment I was too stunned to move, then I hit out at them with my crop. But there were too many of them and I screamed as I felt myself dragged from the saddle. Grinning faces leered at me from all sides. Their hands clawed at me, tearing at my hair. I tasted blood on my lips and I sank to my knees, knowing that this was the end.

"Stop! In God's name stop! Have you no thought for your souls? Kill this woman and you are as guilty as she — and if she be innocent, you are all eternally damned!"

The crowd fell back before the horseman, and I saw that he held a pistol in his hand. His eyes blazed with anger; and the village folk were suddenly quiet. He had an air of command and the bearing of a soldier. Now he had reached me and I struggled to my feet, wiping the blood from my mouth on the sleeve of my gown.

"Are you hurt, Mistress Frome?" he asked.

I shook my head. "I think not, sir — you were just in time."

He surveyed the crowd scornfully.

"Have you no shame? No gratitude for what this woman tried to do for you? If she could not save everyone it was no fault of hers. Some were saved by God's mercy — be thankful for that. Other villages have suffered as greatly, you are not the only ones. How could this woman have brought the sickness? Have you not seen it before?"

"My pond — what about my pond?" cried an old man.

The stranger laughed harshly. "It dried because the rain did not come — God sends the rain, old one, not this woman. Go home, all of you, and pray."

They began to look at one another the dawning of shame in their eyes. I heard them whispering among themselves; then they started to melt away, drifting back to their homes. All save one. He stared at me, the hatred burning as fiercely as ever in his eyes.

"Next time, witch — next time you will not escape," he said. Then he turned and strode off angrily, pushing his way through those who still watched silently.

The stranger dismounted and came to help me mount my horse. "Can you manage to ride?" he asked.

"Yes, I thank you, sir. I am afraid I do not know your name," I said, "though I feel I have seen you before."

He laughed. "Then you have a good memory, Mistress Frome. We met once many years ago. It was when we were children; you called to us . . . "

"And you came but the others made you go with them. Good evening, Tom."

He doffed his hat with its brave feather. "Tom Reynolds at your service, ma'am. I oft wished I had stopped that day. You looked so hurt and I was sorry for it."

I smiled. "Well, you have made up for it today, Tom Reynolds."

He chuckled, a deep, merry sound. "It was a pleasure, ma'am." Then his smile disappeared. "I will see you home. I think it unlikely they will trouble you again today, but it is best to be sure."

"Then I thank you again, sir."

We rode towards Hallows as the sun finally faded from the sky. It was almost dark when we reached the house. He dismounted, coming to lift me down, his strong hands lingering about my waist. I looked at him; he was not a handsome man, except when he smiled, but I owed him my life and his hands were gentle as he set me down.

"Will you come in, Tom?" I asked. "I must wash this filth off and change my gown — but afterwards we will dine together."

He gazed into my eyes and for a moment his hands tightened about my waist. He knew that I was offering him more than the meal and I could see he was tempted. Then he sighed regretfully.

"I thank you, mistress. You are fair and I would like to stay — but I think once a man had you in his blood he would never again be free of you. And I have a good wife who waits for me at home."

"You are wise, Tom Reynolds. Go to your wife and if I can ever be of service to your family you have only to ask."

He made me an elegant bow. "I shall remember."

I smiled. "Then go with God, sir."

"Farewell, mistress. God be with you."

I watched him leave without regret. I had offered lightly, more from gratitude than desire, though it would have been easy to lie with him. I liked his gentle manners and his smile. Somehow he reminded me of Geraint. Yes, it would not have been hard to lie with him. Some would call me wanton and perhaps I am. But if God wanted me to be virtuous — why did he make me the way I am? I need, I hunger, and already I had been alone too long.

9

AFTER my narrow escape from death I found that I no longer cared to ride out alone. I could not forget the look of hatred in the tall man's eyes. So I stayed within the bounds of Hallows and spent my time with Stefan.

These were happy days for me. I had come to love Thérèse's son as dearly as if he were my own. He was so like Justin in every way that he could have been our son if our lives had not been cursed so tragically.

He loved me and thought of me as his mother, but he had not forgotten who or what he was. I had kept my word to Thérèse. I had also tried to tell him about his father, but there I failed, for I knew little of Stefan. So I could only tell him that his father had died bravely for the King and perhaps that was enough for now. It must be for Geraint to tell him the rest, and the time was fast approaching.

I had made no claim for Hallows. Geraint had claimed it in Stefan's name, pressing his rights above Robert's brother with the King. If he succeeded, he might let me continue to live here and care for Stefan as I always had. If he lost his claim I should leave Hallows and Stefan would go to France with his uncle. As for me? I would face that when the time came. I cared little for my own life once Stefan was safe.

* * *

Two months after the incident with the village folk, a messenger came to Hallows. The King had commanded me to present myself at court without delay.

I was taken by surprise, and I had no heart for the journey. But the King's command must be obeyed, so I set about my packing. It was soon done, for I had bothered with no new finery. A red tamine gown that was new when I wed Justin and the orris lace Thérèse had given me would have to suffice. It was not fitting and I could only hope his Majesty would not be offended by my shabby appearance; but there was no time to waste in buying new clothes.

The messenger was to be my escort, and, as we hastened towards the city, it crossed my mind that my situation was a delicate one. I had been a Puritan's wife, in name if not in truth, and I wondered if I might find myself lodged at the tower and not the palace. But my fears were foolish and fled as swiftly as they came.

I was given a small but comfortable room and told to prepare myself to meet the King. I did as I was bidden, putting on the red gown and brushing my hair until it shone. The result was reasonable, I thought — but perhaps that was merely woman's vanity. Then I sat down to wait for the summons to

His Majesty's presence.

A footman came to fetch me. He was dressed in scarlet velvet and gold braid, and his scornful look told me what he thought of my old-fashioned gown. I followed him along endless corridors and up a flight of dimly-lit steps, ending abruptly in a silken drape. He pulled this aside to reveal the door behind and bade me enter.

I went in expecting to see the King, but no one was there, so I began to look about me. It was not a large chamber, but tastefully furnished in the French style so popular since His Majesty's return from that country. But what drew my attention were the pictures lining the walls, some of them by artists I already knew and loved, others new to me. I studied them with interest and so absorbed did I become that I failed to notice another door opening behind me. I jumped when the voice said:

"You admire my pictures, madam?"

I turned to see the tall, graceful

man watching me. He wore a coat and breeches of grey and a blue sash hung across his chest; and pinned to the sash a star of sapphires and diamonds, flashing fire in the candlelight. I curtsied.

"Forgive me, Sire. I did not hear you come in."

He ignored my apology, waving his hand towards the pictures. "My father was a great collector. Unfortunately, many of his pictures have been lost to us — one way or another. However, as you see, we begin again." Then, in a different tone: "We begin again . . . "

I saw the sadness in those deep, slumberous eyes and my heart went out to him for all that he had suffered. "And we who love you, Sire, are truly grateful for it," I said, curtsying reverently.

"And are you among those who love me, Mistress Jalinda?"

I was surprised that he remembered my name. Looking up, I saw that even though he was now a king and had suffered for his crown, his eyes were still as merry when he chose as they had been in childhood.

I smiled. "I have ever loved Your Majesty, as I loved your father before you."

He frowned. "But they told me you married a Puritan — how can this be?"

"It was a matter of survival, Sire." He nodded, understanding as I had known he, of all men, would understand the need to survive. "Besides, I made a bargain with him — and one should always pay one's debts."

"Indeed, madam. I would hear of this bargain."

I told him all, holding nothing back and he listened in silence. "I see," he said, when I had finished. "Faith, madam, I like it not — you and a Puritan! 'Tis a mortal sin."

He was mocking me and thus encouraged, I grew bolder. "Would it please Your Majesty to know that I outwitted him a little?" When he nodded I spoke of my life as Robert's wife, but as I came to the part where I had so misused the Bible, he frowned

"That was not well done of you, madam."

"But, Sire, it was a Puritan directory."

"Ah . . . " he said. "Then that is another matter. You are forgiven, Mistress Jalinda."

I saw a gleam of mischief in his eyes and I laughed. He smiled. "You will surely burn for your wickedness," he said, then grew serious again. "I have received two claims for Hallows — you know this? From the brother of Robert Francis and from your husband's cousin. Yet I have heard nothing from you — do you not wish to claim your husband's estate?"

"No, Sire, 'tis surely Stefan's by right."

"But you did so much to save it — do you not want it for yourself?"

"Nay, Your Majesty. It was for Justin's sake — now he is dead, I care not for Hallows. If I am permitted to remain with my nephew I will do so, if not . . . " I shrugged.

He studied me in silence briefly, then: "You like a bargain, madam. If I give you Hallows and the guardianship of your nephew — what will you give me?"

"Nothing, Sire."

"Nothing?! Oddsfish, madam. You would strike a bargain with a snivelling Puritan — but you will not do the same for your king?"

I trembled, for I had deeply offended him, yet I met his eyes boldly. "But, Sire, he was not a gentleman and had little honour. Methinks you have too much to press a lady when you have the advantage."

"Faith, but you have me there," he replied, laughing ruefully.

I smiled. "Sometimes what cannot be bought may still be freely given. If I knew I was welcome at court I might return in time."

"I like the sound of that better, Mistress Jalinda," he said, smiling at me. "Go home and wait while I decide what fate should best befall a woman who promised her life to a king but gave a goodly part of it to one of his enemies."

"Not gave, Sire — sold." I curtsied once more and prepared to leave, but he detained me.

"How have I offended you, Mistress Jalinda?"

I looked up, startled. "Offended me, Sire? It is I who have perhaps offended you."

He shook his head and I saw his eyes were warm. "No, madam, I must have offended you, for I remember you took leave of me more kindly when last we met."

I blushed, casting down my eyes. "What a lady may dare with a boy, even though he be a prince, she may not aspire to in a king."

He laughed, raising me up so that I looked into his face. "You have a silver tongue, madam — but since the lady is too modest, the king will dare."

So saying he put his arms around me, kissing me soundly just as he had when he was a child, though a little differently, for the prince had become a king, the boy a man. He kissed me lingeringly, with a passion which left me breathless and shaken; then he released me.

"Go home, Mistress Jalinda. I would listen to all before I decide."

I curtsied once more and this time he let me go. But reaching the door, I said softly: "Thank you, Sire."

"For what? I have promised nothing."

I opened the door. "For remembering," I said. I could hear his merry laughter as I closed the door behind me.

★ ★ ★

I returned to Hallows to await what next fate had in store for me. Two months passed and no word came from the King and I began to think that he was offended after all. My heart was heavy as I thought that I might lose my nephew; but fate had one more jest to play.

It was a mild spring day, a faint breeze kissing the hawthorn blossom, and the air filled with the sound of birdsong. I was busy in my still-room all day and it was late when I realised that Stefan had not come back from his ride. At first I was not too anxious, for it was a lovely day, but when it began to grow dark I wondered where he could be. I decided to search for him and had my horse saddled.

I explored Stefan's favourite haunts first, but there was no sign of him. Now I was really worried. Where should I look for him — towards the cliffs or the village? But I had warned him never to go to the village alone. Suddenly I was filled with a terrible fear. Supposing he had disobeyed me — supposing he had actually gone to the village?! The thought made me shake with fear.

"Oh, no! Please, God, don't let it be that!" I cried aloud.

I turned my horse towards the village, digging my heels in hard. I could think of only one thing: the man who hated me lived in that village. What if he had seized the chance to be revenged on me by harming Stefan?

The sun had slipped from the sky now, in its place a silvery moon, showing me the path as I flew over the hard ground. Then, when I was still some distance from the village, I saw the figures clearly outlined against the darkening sky. They were locked in a deathly struggle, the slight, fair youth and the tall, dark man. I saw the man throw the boy to the ground and fall upon him as they rolled over the dry turf. I rode at them furiously, almost falling in my haste to dismount, and I threw myself on the man's back, pulling at his hair and screaming at him to leave Stefan alone.

The man's head jerked up; he swore and brought his shoulder round sharply, dislodging me from his back. The next moment I was pinioned beneath his body, struggling wildly and clawing at his face with my nails.

"Good God! — Jalinda . . . ?"

The sound of his voice made my heart contract and I looked up into his face. "Geraint . . . " I whispered, going limp in his arms.

For a second he stared at me in bewilderment, then he was on his feet, helping me to rise. "Are you hurt? I didn't know it was you . . . "

"We were only fooling, Jalinda." Stefan looked anxiously at my white face. "I met my uncle on the road and we started talking, then . . . I'm sorry if you were frightened."

I was shaking so much that I could hardly take in what he was saying. "Your fight looked so real," I whispered. "I thought, I thought . . . " I got no further. The world span round crazily and for the first time in my life I fainted. When I came to myself again I was in Geraint's arms, held close to his heart while he spoke my name in a way which made me catch my breath.

I smiled at him and for a moment I thought he was going to kiss me and my pulses raced, then his face went cold and he set me down. We stared at each other silently.

"Geraint . . . ?" I broke off, remembering all that lay between us. He was remembering, too.

"Can you ride?" he asked, his voice harsh.

"Yes." I felt stiff, numbed, wanting to bridge the gap between us but knowing it was impossible.

Geraint helped me to mount and we all rode back to Hallows, the silence lengthening into a brittle tension which even Stefan could feel. I knew he liked Geraint and that he was hurt by my apparent restraint. When we parted in the hallway, I to warn Mrs. Beeson that we had a guest, and Stefan to take his uncle up to his room, I felt a reserve in his manner towards me that had never been there before.

When I entered the kitchen Mrs. Beeson looked at me, her sharp eyes noticing my pallor. "What is it?" she asked.

I tried to smile. "We have a visitor — Stefan's uncle."

"What has he done to make you look like that?"

"Nothing — nothing at all."

"Don't lie to me, Jalinda. Do you think I don't know you after all these years?" She was silent for a moment, then: "You love him, don't you?"

"Yes."

"Then tell him so."

"I cannot — you don't understand. You have no idea of what I have done . . . It would shame him to take me as his wife."

She clicked her tongue. "There's not much I don't know about you, Jalinda, but I never thought you were a fool. But that's just what you are if you let him leave without telling him how you feel!"

I blinked back my tears. "It is too late. He hates me."

"Then he's the fool!" she said. "And

335

if I had my way I'd tell him so to his face!"

"Oh, my dear friend, take no notice of my foolishness. It was only the shock of seeing him — I shall be all right in a little while."

"Aye, so you say," she muttered, banging her pots angrily as she worked.

I left her muttering to herself and went up to change my gown. As I dressed, her words kept running through my mind. Was I a fool to let my chance of happiness slip away? Geraint's voice had been tender as he held me in his arms — yet the next moment he had acted as though he hated me. I had made him hate me. I sighed. It was useless to dwell on what might have been. It was too late for regrets.

At the dinner-table I made an effort to act naturally, smiling and asking Geraint questions about his home in France. He seemed surprised at first, then he relaxed and began to talk freely. I watched Stefan's face, seeing his admiration for his uncle reflected there, and I knew that whatever the King's decision regarding Hallows I was going to lose Stefan. When Geraint went back to France the boy would go with him. Well, it was his right to choose; I should not stand in his way.

Geraint had always been able to hold the attention of those who listened to him, soon I found that I was laughing without having to try very hard. Stefan smiled at me and I was well rewarded for the effort I had made. He questioned Geraint endlessly, his face alight with eagerness.

The evening passed swiftly. We sat before the dying embers of the fire until the early hours of the morning. Stefan was reluctant to go to bed even then, and it was only Geraint's insistence that he himself was tired which forced the boy to bid us goodnight at last. When he had gone, there was silence for a moment, then I laughed.

"You have made a conquest, Geraint. I have never seen Stefan so excited."

"Do you mind?" he asked, looking at me strangely.

"Why should I? He is growing up, he needs a man's companionship. I am glad he is happy."

"And you — are you happy?"

"Don't pity me, Geraint. I shall manage without him. You are going to take him with you, aren't you?"

"The King has given you the right to decide, Jalinda. Stefan is your ward; you can keep him here if you wish."

"I am sorry. You must feel very bitter towards me, Geraint. I have denied you your nephew all these years — but I will do so no longer. Stefan must go with you if he wishes. He is not a child any more."

"Why should I be bitter? I claimed Hallows in Stefan's name because you would have had nothing if Robert Francis's brother had won. The estate is yours until Stefan comes of age and afterwards there is provision . . . "

"Why did you do that for me, Geraint?" I asked, watching him closely.

"I owed it to you. You looked after my brother's son — and his wife while she lived . . . "

"But you would have done that, Geraint, had I let you. I do not think you are telling me all the truth."

He frowned. "So you will have it, Jalinda? You will spare me nothing, so be it. I fought for you because I love you — there are you satisfied now?"

"But you hate me — I made you hate me!"

"For a time perhaps. But even while the thought of you with Justin sickened me I understood. And then he told me . . . "

"Justin told you what?" I asked, staring at him.

"It was during the war. He had been drinking heavily. I tried to stop him for his own sake and we quarrelled. He accused me of lying to you and then he told me everything that happened between you. He still wanted you, though he believed you in his heart — that was why he couldn't come home. He knew he would not be able to stay away from your bed — so he stayed away from Hallows."

"I hurt him so badly. It was all my fault."

"But you did not know he was your brother."

"No — though I ought to have guessed. But I did know he was betrothed to Selina and I deliberately set out to take him from her."

"Not without Justin's help. It was no accident that he came to your room that night. Justin was weak; he knew that he did not have the courage to face his father and ask him for you. He believed that once you were with child his father would demand that he marry you."

I stared at Geraint, and I knew that he was right. Justin had been weak, I had learned that long ago. "What you say may be true — but it is only a part of the whole. There is so much you do not know . . . "

"Then tell me, Jalinda."

340

I hesitated, afraid to speak. He said he loved me, but was his love strong enough to accept all I had to tell him? I drew a deep breath, then I began. I told him how the shock of my wickedness had killed my father; I told him of my liaison with Robert during the war, and I told him that I was a witch and had cursed a man to death. He listened in silence until I reached this part of my story and then he smiled.

"Jalinda, Jalinda," he said. "You foolish child. There is no such thing as a witch; it is all superstitious nonsense."

"But he died, Geraint. I cursed him and he died."

"We all die, Jalinda, one way or another. As for this man, after what he did to you, I would have killed him then and there and saved you the trouble!"

"And my father — am I guiltless of his death, too?"

"Sir Ralph was ill; he could not have lived much longer anyway. But here I am as much to blame as you. He wanted to tell you everything so that we could be betrothed at the same time as Thérèse and Stefan — but I begged him to wait. I thought you still a child and I wanted to give you time to grow up. I was wrong. And, before you ask, I knew what you did for Father Renard's sake. He suspected as much, though you lied to ease his conscience."

"Do not endow me with a martyr's crown, Geraint. I did nothing which caused me grief, believe me. I despised Robert — yet I found some pleasure in his arms. I am not a virtuous woman."

"I have always found virtuous women boring. An honest slut makes an easier companion than a saint."

"Geraint!" I cried, laughing and crying simultaneously. "How good you are for me. Why did you not beat some sense into me that day? You were right and I was wrong — you should have carried me off by force."

"I would never do that, Jalinda. I

wanted you to come to me of your own free will — I still do." The look in his eyes turned my knees to water. "Come to France with me — I will teach you to love me."

"I think I always did love you, Geraint. I could not see it because I was blinded by my obsession with Justin. But, when we met again, I saw that you were all I had believed him to be — all that he was not."

He took my hands, looking deep into my eyes. "Think carefully, Jalinda," he said. "I can forget the past as if it had never been — but if you come to me as my wife you will belong to me; and if you ever look at another man with those green eyes of yours I shall kill you."

He was smiling and I knew he was gently mocking me. "If you have no other work for your sword, Geraint, then it will lie idle at your side."

I gazed up into his eyes and I knew I had found peace at last. Geraint loved me for what I was, not what I appeared to be. Others might want me for my beauty and the pleasure I could bring them; but only with this one man could I truly be myself. God had brought him back to me, and in my heart I would thank Him all the days of my life.

"I am not worthy of you, Geraint," I said. "But if you wilt have me, I am yours. Do with me as you will."

His laughter was merry, triumphant. I had thought that smile hateful once, but now it set my pulses racing.

"Do with you as I will, Jalinda? What if I were to take you at your word — now?"

I looked down, demure and innocent. "It shall be as my lord desires."

He laughed again, for pure joy. "Do not become too submissive, Jalinda — I do not think I could bear it."

I raised my eyes to his then, so that he saw all the love and longing reflected there. His eyes burned deep into my soul, seeking and finding the truth. Then, in one, decisive movement, he swept me up in his arms; carrying me up the stairs as though I weighed no more than a feather pillow. He took me to his room, knowing mine held too many memories; and there in that big bed I became more truly a wife than I had ever been.

I knew fulfilment at last. Until this moment I had not understood the meaning of the word. My love for Justin had been a pale candleglow beside the raging fire which consumed me now; with Robert it had been only the fleeting pleasures of the flesh — but with Geraint it was as if our hearts, minds, our very souls were as one. To neither of the others had I truly belonged; but Geraint would be my master and I was content that it should be so.

The chains might be fine and golden, but they would be there and I was glad. It was what I had always needed; a strong man beside me, to love me and guide me in the way I should go. A man on whom I could rely, to whom I could turn when doubts and fears possessed me. A man I could both love and respect. Geraint was all of these things and more.

As we lay side by side, in the languorous aftermath of love, I turned to him and asked: "Am I wicked to take so much pleasure in your love, Geraint? Does my wantonness displease you?"

He laughed. "I always knew you would be so, my love. I knew you were the one woman who could hold and delight me for all of my life. I would have you no other way."

"Oh, Geraint, I do not deserve such happiness! How is it that you understood all those years ago and it took me so long to learn?"

"Perhaps it was meant to be so; I cannot tell. I only know that I will never let you go." Then he saw the jade heart lying against my breast and he touched its smooth surface lightly. "Why did you keep it, Jalinda?"

I smiled. "Father Renard spoke the truth, Geraint. It was my most precious possession. At first I was hurt and angry, but then I began to think. I was sure it was intended as a betrothal token, therefore, your thoughts must have been very different at the start. I came to believe that I knew what you might have meant . . . "

"And what was that, my love?"

I blushed at the tenderness in his eyes. "I thought that in its very simplicity it was a thing of rare beauty — and I wondered if you had been telling me it was how you thought of me."

"I knew you would understand, for our minds were always attuned, even when we quarrelled. It was that and more . . . "

I looked up with the question in my eyes and, seeing the deep glow of his love for me reflected in his face, I felt humbled, unworthy of such love.

"Jade is an enduring stone, Jalinda. It will look as lovely in a hundred years as it does now. It was a symbol of my love for you, which will endure for life itself and perhaps beyond."

I could find no answer to such an avowal and so I merely smiled at him. His hand caressed my breast, slowly tracing the line of my navel; seeking the warm, secret places of my body. My flesh tautened as the delicious pain shot through me and the hot, liquid desire churned inside me once more. I moved beneath him, moaning softly as the fever mounted, making me cry out with joy. Geraint laughed, kissing my eyelids and whispering my name as the tears of happiness ran silently down my cheeks.

Later I asked: "Shall we go to court?"

"Nay, Jalinda. I love and revere the King — but he is too charming and too fond of beautiful women. And you are too beautiful."

I sat up in alarm. "Geraint! You cannot think . . . ?"

I stared at him anxiously; he could not still believe that I would ever again belong to anyone but him? Then I saw that he was teasing me in his old way; he knew, as surely as I, that there would never be another man for me.

"I will take you if you wish," he said, smiling. "But for myself I am weary of the life, of intrigues and the constant struggle for power which must always attend the court. I am no longer young, Jalinda. I would live with you in peace and the hope of a son to follow me."

"I am no longer young either, Geraint. But I am content to be with you and Stefan — and, God willing we shall have sons of our own."

"You will always be young and beautiful to me," he whispered, drawing me into his arms again. I went so willingly, for never had I known such completeness as now.

I would go with him to his land across the sea; our sons would grow tall and bronze like their father and we should grow old together in peace and happiness.

So it was, so it is, and so it shall be. I know and why should I not? For, after all — am I not a witch?

THE END

WITH SOMEBODY ELSE
Theresa Charles

Rosamond sets off for Cornwall with Hugo to meet his family, blissfully unaware of the shocks in store for her.

A SUMMER FOR STRANGERS
Claire Hamilton

Because she had lost her job, her flat and she had no money, Tabitha agreed to pose as Adam's future wife although she believed the scheme to be deceitful and cruel.

VILLA OF SINGING WATER
Angela Petron

The disquieting incidents that occurred at the Vatican and the Colosseum did not trouble Jan at first, but then they became increasingly unpleasant and alarming.

DOCTOR NAPIER'S NURSE
Pauline Ash

When cousins Midge and Derry are entered as probationer nurses on the same day but at different hospitals they agree to exchange identities.

A GIRL LIKE JULIE
Louise Ellis

Caroline absolutely adored Hugh Barrington, but then Julie Crane came into their lives. Julie was the kind of girl who attracts men without even trying.

COUNTRY DOCTOR
Paula Lindsay

When Evan Richmond bought a practice in a remote country village he did not realise that a casual encounter would lead to the loss of his heart.

ENCORE
Helga Moray

Craig and Janet realise that their true happiness lies with each other, but it is only under traumatic circumstances that they can be reunited.

NICOLETTE
Ivy Preston

When Grant Alston came back into her life, Nicolette was faced with a dilemma. Should she follow the path of duty or the path of love?

THE GOLDEN PUMA
Margaret Way

Catherine's time was spent looking after her father's Queensland farm. But what life was there without David, who wasn't interested in her?

HOSPITAL BY THE LAKE
Anne Durham

Nurse Marguerite Ingleby was always ready to become personally involved with her patients, to the despair of Brian Field, the Senior Surgical Registrar, who loved her.

VALLEY OF CONFLICT
David Farrell

Isolated in a hostel in the French Alps, Ann Russell sees her fiancé being seduced by a young girl. Then comes the avalanche that imperils their lives.

NURSE'S CHOICE
Peggy Gaddis

A proposal of marriage from the incredibly handsome and wealthy Reagan was enough to upset any girl — and Brooke Martin was no exception.

A DANGEROUS MAN
Anne Goring

Photographer Polly Burton was on safari in Mombasa when she met enigmatic Leon Hammond. But unpredictability was the name of the game where Leon was concerned.

PRECIOUS INHERITANCE
Joan Moules

Karen's new life working for an authoress took her from Sussex to a foreign airstrip and a kidnapping; to a real life adventure as gripping as any in the books she typed.

VISION OF LOVE
Grace Richmond

When Kathy takes over the rundown country kennels she finds Alec Stinton, a local vet, very helpful. But their friendship arouses bitter jealousy and a tragedy seems inevitable.

CRUSADING NURSE
Jane Converse

It was handsome Dr. Corbett who opened Nurse Susan Leighton's eyes and who set her off on a lonely crusade against some powerful enemies and a shattering struggle against the man she loved.

WILD ENCHANTMENT
Christina Green

Rowan's agreeable new boss had a dream of creating a famous perfume using her precious Silverstar, but Rowan's plans were very different.

DESERT ROMANCE
Irene Ord

Sally agrees to take her sister Pam's place as La Chartreuse the dancer, but she finds out there is more to it than dyeing her hair red and looking like her sister.

HEART OF ICE
Marie Sidney

How was January to know that not only would the warmth of the Swiss people thaw out her frozen heart, but that she too would play her part in helping someone to live again?

LUCKY IN LOVE
Margaret Wood

Companion-secretary to wealthy gambler Laura Duxford, who lived in Monaco, seemed to Melanie a fabulous job. Especially as Melanie had already lost her heart to Laura's son, Julian.

NURSE TO PRINCESS JASMINE
Lilian Woodward

Nick's surgeon brother, Tom, performs an operation on an Arabian princess, and she invites Tom, Nick and his fiancé to Omander, where a web of deceit and intrigue closes about them.

THE WAYWARD HEART
Eileen Barry

Disaster-prone Katherine's nickname was "Kate Calamity", but her boss went too far with an outrageous proposal, which because of her latest disaster, she could not refuse.

FOUR WEEKS IN WINTER
Jane Donnelly

Tessa wasn't looking forward to meeting Paul Mellor again — she had made a fool of herself over him once before. But was Orme Jared's solution to her problem likely to be the right one?

SURGERY BY THE SEA
Sheila Douglas

Medical student Meg hadn't really wanted to go and work with a G.P. on the Welsh coast although the job had its compensations. But Owen Roberts was certainly not one of them!

HEAVEN IS HIGH
Anne Hampson

The new heir to the Manor of Marbeck had been found. But it was rather unfortunate that when he arrived unexpectedly he found an uninvited guest, complete with stetson and high boots.

LOVE WILL COME
Sarah Devon

June Baker's boss was not really her idea of her ideal man, but when she went from third typist to boss's secretary overnight she began to change her mind.

ESCAPE TO ROMANCE
Kay Winchester

Oliver and Jean first met on Swale Island. They were both trying to begin their lives afresh, but neither had bargained for complications from the past.

CASTLE IN THE SUN
Cora Mayne

Emma's invalid sister, Kym, needed a warm climate, and Emma jumped at the chance of a job on a Mediterranean island. But Emma soon finds that intrigues and hazards lurk on the sunlit isle.

BEWARE OF LOVE
Kay Winchester

Carol Brampton resumes her nursing career when her family is killed in a car accident. With Dr. Patrick Farrell she begins to pick up the pieces of her life, but is bitterly hurt when insinuations are made about her to Patrick.

DARLING REBEL
Sarah Devon

When Jason Farradale's secretary met with an accident, her glamorous stand-in was quite unable to deal with one problem in particular.

THE PRICE OF PARADISE
Jane Arbor

It was a shock to Fern to meet her estranged husband on an island in the middle of the Indian Ocean, but to discover that her father had engineered it puzzled Fern. What did he hope to achieve?

DOCTOR IN PLASTER
Lisa Cooper

When Dr. Scott Sutcliffe is injured, Nurse Caroline Hurst has to cope with a very demanding private case. But when she realises her exasperating patient has stolen her heart, how can Caroline possibly stay?

A TOUCH OF HONEY
Lucy Gillen

Before she took the job as secretary to author Robert Dean, Cadie had heard how charming he was, but that wasn't her first impression at all.